Dream of Me

by

Seven Rodgers

Dedication

For Terri and Brenda Franks (rip Brenda)

Acknowledgements

Gratitude to my editors Joe Lee, Tami Jeffers, and Ally Robertson who buffed and polished this book.

Much love to my son, Luke Poulsen, who believes in my vision and in his "ole' Ma.

Camille Breen explained that senior love isn't as easy as I thought. That got my juices going and sent Dream of Me in a whole different direction. Thank you, my dear friend.

Chapter One

"My marriage was like riding a tricky racehorse," Jozelyn said to her friends as they sat outside a deli in Fernandina Beach, Florida, enjoying the bay breeze that cooled the sun-scorched cobblestone street. "Sometimes galloping—then, boom, screeching to a halt. The steed I met years before turned into a bucking bronco. He stomped on me until I became physically and emotionally crippled."

She paused, rubbing away the odd headache she had nursed all morning and raised a glass of lemonade in a toast to them. "And you guys supported me through all of that."

"Joz, you didn't marry a thoroughbred. You married an ass." Cammy snickered. Cammy, the respected, oldest member of the group, was a mentor to mistreated women, sponsoring Joz for many years. "Discernment isn't your forte."

"True enough but it wasn't completely his fault," Joz muttered. "Y'all know how ADD I am. Focusing without distraction, remembering dates, and incorrectly hearing others makes life problematic enough without an insensitive, demeaning husband adding to it. I promise in front of all of you, I won't ever marry again—enough is enough."

"Joz," Cammy continued. "Relationships always are a two-way street as you learned long ago. Oh, Emma is

1

new and shared that she would like you to explain your 'life strategy.' "

Jozelyn's friends chuckled before she spoke.

"Well, it's not a plan at all," she said. "I step forward and land. I make the best of whatever situation I'm given until it's time to move on. I start over and arrive somewhere else, whether it's a different job or relationship." She raised her glass again. "I call it the ADD Hopscotch—Forrest Gump has nothing on me. Somehow, I meet awesome people despite landing on my unsure feet, and you ladies always think that explanation is funny."

"Oh, you've overcome a lot, Jozelyn, and we commend you for it," Cammy said. "Your situation isn't amusing, but you share your difficulties with a lighthearted delivery. Tell us more."

She fiddled with her napkin that the salty breeze threatened to carry away. "Well, ADD brains include problems with making decisions. I can't set a goal and stick to it like you guys. Instead, I set blurry intentions, and that brings me surprising and, sometimes, uncomfortable situations. Especially with choices in work, former boyfriends, and in my marriage."

Joz paused. All of them, Emma included, were listening attentively.

"Go on," Cammy said.

"Not much more to tell. After all these years I've learned to handle my flaws, so I function without anxiety ruling every minute of my life. Most people don't understand my struggle—I appear ditzy to people at times, especially when I can't make up my mind about something. But I've accepted myself, and I hope you do too, even if you find me worth a giggle … it's okay."

She was gearing up to share some big news: she had listed her house and would leave Amelia Island to start over elsewhere. She needed a new start, and her Realtor said an almost immediate sale for a healthy profit was as likely as the sun coming up in the morning.

Silently some friends thought it was too soon to make a change after a divorce. Others rallied around to support her decision to move to St. Croix in the United States Virgin Islands. Cammy kept silent, knowing Joz would do what Joz wanted to do. She threw a bon voyage party at her house the weekend before Joz left, wondering if Joz could handle a solitary life so far away.

****

Joz entered the airport with one thought. *I was courageous in my twenties. I sure hope that strength resurfaces and helps me handle a seismic shift now.*

Chapter Two

Joz slept peacefully the first night in her new home. But as the morning sun appeared on the horizon, she jolted awake as a cacophony of noise hit her ears from what sounded like thousands of chickens and roosters.

"Wonderful," she muttered, before padding into the kitchen for coffee. "That's a sound I'll have to grow used to."

Heating a cup of water in the microwave, she stirred in a heaping tablespoon of Folgers with cream before heading to the Juliette balcony. She sipped her drink before propping her feet up on the railing that gave way. Her chair rocked forward almost spilling her to the ground two stories below.

Crap, she thought, her heart pounding. *I forgot the inspection did mention the loose railing. Well, I did buy a fixer upper, and this fix is first on my list.*

After making a second cup, she again sat on the balcony carefully avoiding the unprotected edge. She stared at the horizon where the heavens blended into the cobalt-blue sea, casting a sense of unity and peacefulness. Dawn skies of oranges and pinks, swirled Picasso-like while tropical breezes prodded cartoon clouds that floated by like a parade. Jozelyn sighed happily enjoying the natural world around her. Iguanas and deer played peek-a-boo from the woods by the house. A mongoose zipped by. Joz broke into a smile. I could stay here for eternity.

It may take an eternity to fix this house.

Chapter Three

Eight Months Later

The island's only twelve-step program scheduled their meetings downtown too late in the evening for Joz. She missed the honesty and companionship of Al-Anon friends but kept in touch through texting and social media. She made few acquaintances in St. Croix having difficulty understanding the East Indian dialect, but the only thing she really felt lacking was artistic inspiration and that was on her, choosing to deal with the needs of the house before her own happiness that included an active involvement in the arts.

No wonder I've been feeling blue in paradise.

She hurried inside and grabbed the thin island newspaper delivered to her door. Sipping coffee while thumbing her way through it, she spotted an advertisement for an evening show at a downtown art gallery. This, finally, spurred her creative juices, but the self-doubt that plagued her during those awful years with the taskmaster she married began to hold her down like a heavy weight on her shoulders.

"Come on, stop floundering," she said to her dresser mirror that evening. "You need to experience something different. You are smart and industrious, no matter what your ex thought. You can mingle if you must."

An internal voice countered that it was hardly ideal to arrive alone at an artistic event since she had become a reclusive sort, but how else would she meet local artists?

She decided on her mauve lace dress, thinking it was modest enough for her fifty-eight years. Platform sandals added two inches to her five foot five. She opened a sealed box of makeup and was careful not to overdo it. Finally, she chose a lipstick that blended with her natural, tanned face adding a dash of light, delicate perfume. A decorative seahorse clip held her blond hair in place.

It's been almost a year since I went out. I feel like a girl playing dress-up.

"Not bad. I'm no beauty queen, but I'd say I'm attractive for my age with a bit of paint." Joz smiled at herself in the mirror. "Now, do not act like a wallflower. No one will notice you or bother to say hello if you do."

She quelled the nerves that threatened to take over with a deep breathing technique she had learned on an Amelia Island Al-Anon retreat.

I can do this.

****

As the radio blared seventies rock and roll, the Land Rover handled a spirited drive that wound downward past hills of pastureland to the gallery in the center of Christiansted. Driving the SUV on the left side of the road had become second nature, and Joz enjoyed the fresh air blowing through her open windows. She slowed as she entered the main harbor-front town on the east island side, searching for a parking space that she expected to find easily after business hours.

"Oh, come on," she muttered. "Not one space close to the gallery? Now I'm going to be late."

Chapter Four

After crawling through the narrow Christiansted streets, Joz found a spot several blocks from the gallery. She hustled on foot over the uneven sidewalks, slipping into the building fifteen minutes after the exhibit's opening.

The gallery's floors were wood, and the high ceiling exposed mahogany beams that were clearly in place centuries before Denmark sold St. Croix to the United States. Art enthusiasts filled the room listening to the curator explain the charity and cause behind the evening event. Joz caught her breath and settled into the crowd but began to fidget within minutes.

Why do I feel like someone is staring at me?

She fanned herself with a program, carefully inspecting the people paying close attention to the curator's speech. The attendees appeared to be mostly couples, but for some reason she couldn't shake the feeling she was being observed.

Joz finally dared a glance to her left, and there—standing by himself and smiling at her—was a handsome, man's-man type. She guessed he was her age, but he appeared to have a youthful body. When their eyes met, she smiled and gave him a slight nod breathing deeply to slow her racing heart. When focusing on the speaker didn't hold her attention, she tried to concentrate on the program. It was printed on expensive paper and full-color, with information about—

"Good evening."

Joz whirled toward the deep voice. The man whose eyes she'd met moments ago was six feet and wore khakis, a short-sleeve shirt, and boat shoes. His brown hair hadn't turned all gray, but his face showed the lines and character of someone who'd lived longer than her almost fifty-nine years. His deep blue eyes took her breath away and sent goosebumps sprouting across her arms.

"Good evening," he said. "I'm Frank Loveland." His mellow voice was soothing. "I am alone, but I find art more pleasurable with company. Would you care to join me after this intolerable windbag finishes her lecture?"

Joz, feeling the same way, let a giggle slip. His accent struck her as upper-class English. She leaned up to him, not wanting to disturb the people around her. "I'm Jozelyn, but most people call me Joz. It would be fun to enjoy the exhibition together," she heard herself say.

"Shall we break the ice with a drink?"

"Uh, sure … white wine, please."

Frank's smile nearly melted her. An internal voice told her to keep her hormones in check; a second countered by asking if she had any hormones left. Frank walked over to the bar, spoke to the bartender, and returned with a glass of wine filled to the brim.

"You must be a surgeon," she said. "I've never seen such steady hands."

"Shh," the person next to her snapped.

Joz mouthed an apology, which was ignored. Frank

stepped to her side, cutting her off from the irritated patron. "The bartender poured quite enthusiastically. Shall I hold it while you take a sip?"

"That sounds like a plan." The wine tasted lovely, unlike most brands served at local events Joz had attended—it tasted expensive.

"Have some more so it doesn't spill."

Joz felt childish for allowing someone else to hold her glass while she drank. Was this Frank Loveland being playful, or was intimacy on his mind?

"Oh, my, I haven't had wine for a while, but I could get used to this."

Her fingers grazed his as she took the glass from him. She couldn't believe what was happening—after the better part of a year leading a most solitary existence, she'd ventured out at the last minute to an art gallery, not knowing a soul, and a gorgeous man found her almost instantly? Was she dreaming?

She felt intrigued—scared was probably more like it—and was aware of her heart pounding again. She felt physical strength oozing from Frank like a gentle electric current as he held the glass for her. She had another swallow, causing the loudest of her internal voices reminding her not to drink the wine too fast. And how much did this Frank drink? Her ex, even when things were good, drank early and often.

Finally, the curator's drone ended. Voices suddenly swirled around the room, and Joz felt an overload of sound—conversing was now impossible. Frank's voice next to her was almost lost in the mishmash of tones and frequencies.

"It's deafening, don't you think?"

She looked at him, wondering if he was a mind

reader. "I don't hear well with the noise around me."

"Conversation is not a necessity." Frank leaned close to her ear, sending a shiver down her spine. "Shall we?" He offered Joz the crook of his arm. She took it nervously, gulping wine while he finished his drink. "Let's refill first," he said.

"Of course."

Frank led Joz to the portable bar. The bartender nodded and reached into a cooler on the floor. "I drink my personal wine," Frank said, anticipating her question.

"You bring a bottle?"

"Certainly. Art functions serve questionable brands of wine."

"Oh, yes, I agree totally. Usually they sour my stomach, so I hesitated when you asked if I wanted a drink."

The gallery presented mixed mediums from various local artists. Most were ordinary, but world-class levels of expertise were sprinkled among the lesser efforts. Frank and Joz ambled by them together, winding around the small rooms without chatting but lingering on exceptional pieces that appealed to them both.

"It seems we enjoy the same ones, Joz."

"I enjoy quality art that speaks to me no matter what medium."

"Then, we are two of a kind in the art department."

Beginning to feel a strong physical attraction to this man, Joz breathed deeply, forgetting her commitment to the words "never again." *He loves art.*

Sculptures were mixed throughout the collection of watercolors, acrylics, and oils. Christ carrying the cross sculpted in marble caught Joz's eye. Frank studied it from different angles.

"This piece is exceptional," he said.

"Oh, yes. How did the artist manage to show the brutality in such beautiful work?"

"That is what makes it extraordinary. The beauty of the message remains while showing the intensity of the sacrifice." Frank bent to scrutinize the piece, running his finger lightly over the scars.

"Oh, dear, it costs thousands," Joz said, reading the caption below the sculpture. "That's understandable, but financially out of my league."

"It will grow in value. The sculptor, Surgian, has made quite a name for himself. I must add this rare find to my collection. Would you excuse me while I speak to the curator?"

"Yes, of course."

"Care for another glass?"

"No, thank you. I get tipsy much too fast."

Frank caught the curator and hurried to speak to her. Watching, Joz wondered if he was haggling about the asking price when the curator turned her way, smiled, and nodded. After Frank returned to her, she once again picked up that strong energy he emitted as he took her elbow.

"Shall we move on, Joz?"

Are you going to tell me if you bought the sculpture? "Uh, sure."

****

"Joz, after I finish purchasing my pieces, please join me for dinner."

He is buying the artwork. "Well... I don't usually eat this late." Oh, for God's sake, why did I say that?

"Please keep me company. Order an appetizer or a drink... coffee."

"All right. I'll wait on this interesting bench while you finish your business." She watched as Frank removed a bankroll from the inside pocket of his sport coat while enjoying a refurbished church pew painted in turquoise with gold trim. She couldn't believe he carried enough cash with him to pay for the sculpture, and the curator, she noticed, looked thrilled.

"I apologize for your wait," he said minutes later. "They aren't used to taking cash these days."

"Don't apologize. But what piece did you buy?"

"Pieces, you mean. I shall keep that a secret until you view them in my home."

Hmm. "Aren't you getting ahead of yourself, Frank? I've agreed to supper with you. That's all."

"Ha. Quite right, but I shall stick to my gut feeling about you, Joz. My instincts are never wrong."

"Let's enjoy dinner but not think beyond. It makes me uncomfortable."

Smiling, Frank held the door for her as they stepped outside into the cool but humid night air. "Fair enough, I shall keep my dreams to myself," he said. "How about seafood for dinner?"

"That sounds great." He sounds so incredibly formal.

"Do you usually prefer fish?"

"It's lighter and healthier than meat, although truth be told, I enjoy a steak or homemade pot roast on rare occasions. But it seems the more I mature, the less red meat I want."

"Ah, another commonality between us," Frank said. "I found a talented chef on the east end at Salty Pond Inn. May I share my favorite place with you, Joz?"

"That sounds fun and interesting. Should I meet you

at the restaurant?"

"No, I will drive you as a gentleman should."

Joz tried not to show her concern. "It's a good way from here…"

"Joz, allow me to be a gentleman, please."

He could be a serial killer for all I know—but what serial killer would have spent that kind of money on art and leave with me in front of everyone if he planned on killing me?

"Okay." She looked up at him. "I'll ride with you."

Chapter Five

Frank opened the door to his silver Jeep. Joz climbed inside with her mind vacillating between images of assassins and nice men. She left the imaginings and worked to her center, saying the word "trust" repeatedly in her head while focusing on the custom leather seats and speakers playing Spanish ballads. She was startled when he lowered the volume.

"I don't need to worry about you, right?"

"Excuse me?" What kind of question is that?

"You aren't a thief, or wanted by the law?"

"What? Of course not, ha." A giggle escaped her.

"You find me amusing, do you, dear Joz?"

"Oh, I'm working on my trust issues—I was wondering the same thing about you."

He pulled the Jeep over at a scenic spot. "Let's get something straight from the get-go, lovely woman. I am not a mass murderer, rapist, or serial killer. I already respect you, and I hope to earn your trust in the future."

"I guess I am feeling a little fearful. I must be carrying baggage from my marriage, burdens I had thought were overcome."

"I hope to ease your fears. Quite a view, isn't it?"

The city of Christiansted lit the valley while a vessel's running lights blinked red as it passed the town, heading to the south-end port. A tugboat's low bellow echoed throughout the hills, breaking the stillness of the night.

"It's a wonderful overlook, Frank. Thank you for sharing it with me."

"Right, we better watch the time."

Frank moved back into traffic and drove fast and confidently, handling the curves like a professional. "Why do you smile so, Joz?"

"Most men I've met seem to get their driver's license at Walmart. But I feel comfortable with your expertise."

He laughed. "Thank you, I think. Walmart, huh—men driving that badly?"

"You better believe it."

****

Joz's heart sank as only three cars remained in the parking lot that fronted The Salty Pond Inn. Next door sat a large Crucian inn that matched the restaurant's deep golden yellow with dark-gray shutters. "Are we late?"

"Not at all. I called ahead."

Sure enough, the maître d' met them at the door. "Goodnight, Mr. Loveland."

"Goodnight, Rodolpho. I brought company."

"Excellent, sir. My lady."

Joz smiled, surprised at yet another island salutation. Saying "goodnight" instead of "good evening" still startled her.

"Your table awaits," Rodolpho said with a Spanish accent, leading them to a two-top with an eastern view of Buck Island.

"The chef cooks to order—pan, broiled, or deep-fried," Frank said.

"I'm partial to deep-frying, but I must watch my

cholesterol."

"I understand that battle, but I refuse the medications for it. You haven't enjoyed the inn before, Joz?"

"No, I haven't. This menu offers an amazing selection."

"I usually order The Admiral. It's a selection of fresh fish, scallops, and shrimp."

"That sounds wonderful, but like I said, I don't eat heavily at night."

"Then take the rest home to enjoy tomorrow, my love."

My heart is melting. Joz had heard female servers use "my love" with patrons on St. Croix, but the endearment coming from a man felt extra special after years of emotional abuse.

"Then I'll trust your judgment and order The Admiral."

Frank turned to Rodolpho. "Two of my usual, please."

"Very good, sir."

The maître d' hurried into the kitchen. Within minutes, a short, plump server named Junee delivered two side salads with a generous portion of pepper sprinkled on top. Joz pulled at the mixed greens, thinking she would have an asthma attack if any of the pepper landed in her throat, and knew she looked like a miner scraping away earth in a search for something valuable.

"You don't care for pepper?" Frank asked, reading her mind once again. "I should have asked—I like it loaded."

"I love pepper, but it doesn't love me, so I'm very—"

Disaster struck as a piece of coarse pepper caught in her throat. She grabbed her water glass and gulped, but it was too late.

Damn it, I left the inhaler at home.

Pushing her chair from the table, she got to her feet while covering her mouth with one hand. She trotted to the powder room and made it inside before exploding into a nasty coughing fit, her throat slowly constricting.

Breathe, Joz. Relax. And turn on the spigot—get the water hot.

The hot tap didn't work. Frank stuck his head into the restroom but quickly backed out the door. Joz felt her heart sink at his cowardice, but he returned a minute later with a steaming cup of water. Joz nodded and took it in both hands, inhaling the steam before taking a tiny sip. Her body gradually understood as she repeated the process in a desperate attempt to open her airway.

Finally.

"Frank... I'm so sorry... I'm mortified."

"You mustn't apologize for an illness, ever. Besides, darling, your ability not to panic amazes me, and coming to your rescue makes me feel heroic."

"Well, you are that for sure," Joz said, leaning against the wall.

"Better?"

"Worn out. I'd like to go home. I'll call a cab."

"Like hell you will," Frank said gently but firmly. He took her arm and led her to a chair in the foyer. "I brought you here, and I shall take you home." He called Junee over and requested to-go containers. "Oh, and Chef? A word, please?"

Joz watched Frank march into the kitchen like he owned the restaurant. She closed her eyes, breathing slowly and grateful the crisis had passed, and opened them when she heard two sets of footsteps. The chef was following Frank and held an inhaler in his hand!

"Don't worry," Frank said to her. "I soaked the mouthpiece in hundred-proof alcohol."

"Yes, and he tasted quite a bit of it," the chef winked. He was a tall, thin man, and Joz almost couldn't suppress a laugh when it occurred to her that with his tall, white hat, the chef looked like a human Q-tip. She closed her eyes and inhaled three times before offering the inhaler back to the chef.

"You'll need to disinfect it again," she said, embarrassed. "I so appreciate your kindness, Chef, and yours, too, Frank."

"Please, keep the inhaler in case you need it, Madame. I keep a drawer filled with them in the kitchen and at home. I insist."

Frank sat next to Joz. "Stay at the inn for the night. Chef checked on room availability. Your voice sounds frail, and you look pale as a ghost."

I wish. I dumped all my cash into the house, and this month's bills are due. "That's financially impossible right now. You both have been so kind—"

"That pepper is my fault, Joz," Frank said. "The expense won't dent my bank account, I assure you."

Joz nodded. I want nothing but sleep. It would be ideal.

****

Joz leaned on Frank's arm as they walked across the parking lot to the inn, where the clerk greeted Frank with a huge smile and a key. A small elevator carried them to the third floor and opened to a vast suite filled with rattan furniture and sea pictures on the cream-colored walls.

He can't think I'll share a room with him… can he?

"This is a two-bedroom suite," Frank said. "You stay in the one to the left, and I shall sleep on the far end. But keep your door ajar in case you experience another attack. That way I shall hear if you need help."

Shall I trust him? "Okay. Thank you, Frank."

The air conditioning was running wide open as Joz drew a warm bath, something she missed in the tropics where water came at a premium. The bath would relax her after the inhaler spiked her pulse rate. Another rare headache eased as she sank into the warm water. She smelled Frank's food reheating but was too tired to be hungry. Before she fell asleep in the tub, she climbed out and wrapped herself in a towel. Tiptoeing to bed, she discovered a cup on the end table with a note.

CHAMOMILE TEA, HONEY, AND WHISKEY TO HELP YOU SLEEP, MY LOVE. NO NEED TO WORRY—NOT LACED WITH ROOFIES. FRANK

A smiley face followed. Joz smiled and sniffed the tea, shrugged, and took a sip. "Not bad. What a thoughtful man." And a muscled man had taken the time to draw the smiley face?

Cute was the word that came to mind as she climbed naked under the covers after finishing the cup. She felt comfortable and, oddly, unafraid.

Chapter Six

Joz awoke to the sun peeking through the wood louver shades. She stretched and hopped out of bed to use the bathroom, thinking of the night before. What would Frank say to her? Would he want to see her again? She had to admit that he'd been a perfect gentleman all evening, and he'd left her completely alone once she'd gone to bed.

She worked the tangles from her hair and tried to make it presentable, securing it with the hair clip. She used the toothpaste and disposable toothbrush provided by the hotel, trying to work quickly. Could she call a cab and sneak out before Frank Loveland roused and save herself the embarrassment of looking like something the cat dragged in? Then she smelled coffee and knew it was too late to escape. Frank had seen me at my worst last night and deserved to see the rest of the train wreck.

She stepped into her dress, puffed on the inhaler, and rinsed her mouth again before strolling barefoot into a tiny kitchen that gleamed with stainless steel appliances and a marble countertop. "Good morning, sunshine," Frank said, his deep voice rumbling. "You appear wonderfully refreshed, but you must be starving."

He'd already set a table outside on the balcony. The early morning light reflected off the sea in shades of turquoise and cobalt blue. They stood quietly, admiring the sea's beauty.

"Good morning to you," she said. "I never tire of this view."

"Oh, it is quite the masterpiece. Now, I have made coffee, toasted bran muffins, and ordered soft-boiled eggs. Or would you prefer something else?"

"That sounds delicious. What a lovely table," Joz said, noting seafoam green dishes and cloth napkins to match. "This inn decorates tastefully. And no one's readied breakfast for me since I was a child."

"Good God, who have you been associating with all these years?"

He was smiling, but she gave a serious answer: "That's a deep question. I had a history of meeting characters who didn't have character."

"Ah. That would be the source of your distrusting nature."

"Old habits die hard for me. Please don't take it personally."

"Stuff and nonsense, my love. I shall prove your assumptions wrong, and I love a challenge. Cream and sugar?"

"Just cream, please."

Frank slid out a chair for her, then fixed her a cup of coffee. She closed her eyes after the first, magical sip. "Am I dreaming? This is heavenly."

"It should be." Frank refilled his own cup. "Organic coffee from Colorado."

"Don't English people drink tea for breakfast?"

"We love our tea, but I enjoy strong coffee with real cream for mornings." Frank carefully spread orange marmalade on his muffin. It was her favorite flavor, but what had her attention was how his arms glowed a deep bronze from the sun, showing off taut tendons and muscles."

"Joz?"

"Yes?"

"You went away on me. I asked if you like marmalade."

"I sure do, and that's my favorite. I searched all over the island and never found any."

"I special order it through the restaurant; it's from Florida—again, organic. The Inn uses it, too."

"Does everyone find you interesting and so kind, Frank Loveland?"

The words had popped out as if they had a mind of their own. She braced herself, unsure how he would respond to what, for her, was a forward comment. He smiled and stared into her eyes with a softness that enchanted her.

"Joz, I traveled all my adult life for work. I had no opportunity to settle down, enjoy a family, or anything else that required stability. But those days end soon." He leaned forward, but not enough to invade her personal space, as her Al-Anon friend, Cammy, was fond of saying. "I plan to enjoy my retirement with a pleasant, intelligent woman. I wasn't looking for beauty, but with you, I get all three. I have come too far down the road to beat around the bush—I should like to know you better. And quickly."

He thinks I'm beautiful. I must be dreaming. "Even after you saw me at my absolute worst?"

"If that's your worst, I shall consider myself doubly lucky." He lifted his coffee cup as if in a toast to her as the breeze blew a patch of his hair straight up. It fell like a feather into place as the breeze slowed.

"Frank, you seem to be an incredibly decent man, so you deserve a comprehensive disclosure," she said. "Afterward, you can let me know if you still feel so fortunate."

She saw a change in his body language, a subtle one. "I'm listening."

"In my teens, I broke a vertebra falling off a horse, and it wasn't doctored. Before that, I dove into a shallow pool … twice, landing on my head. My spine is arthritic, top to bottom with nerve damage. From what I've seen of you and your amazing physique, a younger woman or a healthier one might be more suitable—ah, what do you find so funny?"

Frank's coffee almost came back out through his nose as he stifled an outburst. "You dove into a shallow pool twice?"

"I thought changing the angle of my dive would work. I was wrong—very wrong."

"A perfectionist. What age were you?"

"Eleven or twelve. I had an ancient neck and spine by the time I was thirty. Swimming allows me to exercise, the only kind I'm able to do. So, I moved to St. Croix—year-round swimming on uncrowded beaches. I've developed some strength, and it helps keep the weight down if I avoid carbs. I eat lots of protein and fruit too." Joz hesitated, then pushed forward with the rest. "And to top it off, I'm ADD and suffer from occasional PTSD dreams. I'm a mess, a real train wreck."

"Ah." Frank buttered another muffin. He didn't look distressed.

"Men think of my weaknesses as high maintenance. I understand that, although I pride myself on my independence. But I appreciate your company at the art show and for taking care of me. I won't forget it."

"Assisting you was my pleasure, and I shall remember the carbs in the future. But if you don't mind my saying so, you don't see yourself realistically, do you?"

"Excuse me?" Joz heard the edge in her voice. "I admit my failings all too well."

"You look at your afflictions as deal breakers when it comes to potential partners. Do not put all men in the same basket of those you have had before."

His smile was kind. She managed to bite back a tart response.

"Five years your senior helps me to understand some of your pain," he continued. "I deal with arthritic symptoms from age and injuries after an active youth, and though I enjoy excellent health, I feel the years catching up to me."

"But that's just it, Frank. Time catches up to you now at the usual age it touches everyone. My health problems crippled my pace and style in my late forties. I've had decades dealing with my afflictions."

"So, you want an equal balance in physical stamina or lack thereof, but it doesn't exist, Joz. What you endure in bodily weaknesses, you counteract with your cheerful countenance, agreeability, and honesty. Those qualities count—they matter to me." He leaned forward and took her hand. She felt the same electric current she did last night. "We met, two singles in a crowded room. We enjoyed art together; we centered on the same pieces. And two people who love orange marmalade instead of strawberry and grape as most people do? We also share that. Might I ask you an important question?"

"Uh, sure…"

"Do my age and arthritic injuries turn you off?"

"What—of course not!"

"Then why do you think yours would disgust me?"

"My experience I suppose."

"Let me guess. An abusive ex-husband, probably a selfish fool who didn't appreciate what he had? A man-child who thought he was so wonderful that he deserved unblemished women who he treated as eye candy and property?"

"Wow," Joz said, honestly impressed and a bit unnerved. "If you add alcoholic, you're spot on."

"You had parents and or siblings that either neglected or undermined you instead of building up your self-worth?"

She sipped the orange juice, patted her mouth with the napkin, and abruptly pushed her chair from the table. Standing by the railing, she stared at the ocean and breathed deeply. How could this man be so intuitive, this real?

"Please accept my apology," Frank said quickly behind her. "My bluntness upset you. That certainly was not my intention."

"Don't apologize. It's unnerving for a stranger to know me so well. I suppose I've become hard and untrusting, but at my age, Frank, change requires energy I don't have."

He placed his hands on her shoulders and slowly turned her around. "Joz, please allow me to show you what it is to be appreciated, loved, and—above all else—treated with respect." He lifted her chin upward. "Let me be your muse… and your trusted friend."

He leaned close. Joz's heart pounded as he planted

a soft kiss on her cheek. She tried to process what she'd just heard. Again, wondering if she was an actress in a melodramatic dream.

"All right, I'll give you that opportunity—on one condition."

"Name it."

Joz hesitated for a moment to build up courage.

"I've found that a kiss reveals the true nature of a person, and I admit I've been wondering what it would be like to kiss you. So, if you want to …"

He didn't hesitate. Pulling her close, he kissed her lips firmly yet sensuously. He groaned and she was surprised at how eager she was to be held like this, to have this handsome, mysterious man command such an intense physical reaction in her after so many months alone.

Frank suddenly broke the kiss and stepped back. Stunned, she found his eyes and waited for an explanation.

"I am doing everything in my power not to overstep your boundaries," he said, his voice hoarse, "but our lips, our bodies meld. Did you feel it? Or did our kiss disappoint?"

She stepped into his arms, trying to steady her breathing. "Frank, I've never experienced a kiss like that in my entire life. Disappointed? Uh, no. Not at all."

"Then you won't mind if I kiss you again… and again?"

He lightly kissed her cheeks, her neck, and finally pulled her close. Their lips grazed, each tasting a willingness that melted her guard, including the need to be appropriate, or a lady. He kissed her fully, pulling her body impossibly close.

Joz ran her fingers through his hair and down his spine. She pulled his hips, encouraging him. Like he needs it. He effortlessly picked her up and carried her into the bedroom. They removed one another's clothing nervously before they lay on his bed kissing—his erection between her thighs.

"Are you sure, Jozelyn?"

"Yes, I'm sure," she said breathlessly. "But it's been unused for a long time… I'm not certain it works."

He touched her vagina. She felt zapped by a bolt of current. "You feel ready. But I shall be careful."

He entered her slowly, teasing her, moving deeper. She gasped, astonished at the size and depth that was filling her. She heard herself moan as he began to move rhythmically. Her eyes closed, she felt herself let go as he kissed her lips, her face, her ears. Her orgasm rushed through her just as Frank exploded too.

Oh, God, that was incredible. And it had to be good for him—his heart is still pounding. "Frank, what a wonder you are," Joz murmured.

"We also match in bed, my love," he said, catching his breath. "But next time I'll try to take it slower."

"Next time?" She opened her eyes and ruffled his hair. "I'm still enjoying the afterglow for, honestly, the first time in my life."

Gently pushing from him, she slid out of bed and stood on wobbly legs before disappearing into the bathroom. He reached for her when she returned and pulled her into a tight embrace. "Shall we give it another go?" he asked.

This time was just as sweet, and the amazing part was how her mind didn't wander. No anxiety, no nothing—just pure bliss. Yes, that's the right word. He caressed her arms and neck, kissed her breasts, then slid his face to her stomach—before looking up and into her eyes.

"Joz, I have already fallen for you. You have totally won me over and cannot make me leave. Patience is my middle name."

She felt warm, happy tears in her eyes. *Nothing like this has ever happened to me.* "Are you sure, Frank?"

"I am more certain about you than I have ever been about anyone in my entire life. Please allow me to care for you, Joz, to make you happy."

"Oh, Frank…"

"Were I impulsive, I would move you in with me today. Would you consider that possibility for the future?"

"You've worn me out completely, and you expect me to think?"

He chuckled. "Having a hard time switching gears to rational thought?"

"Well, I must admit we're pretty compatible… the bedroom, art, orange marmalade…"

"Yes, orange marmalade is very important."

She giggled and kissed him, then propped herself on an elbow and looked into the eyes of the ravishing older man who swept her off her feet in a period of, what, twelve hours?

"Yes," she said. "Yes, I'd like to date you and spend time together with the possibility of a future, but I stress the word possibility."

He fluffed up his pillows and sat against them. "Fair enough, Jozelyn Hardt. Let's begin—tell me about your days."

"Well… I spend my time leisurely and swim a lot. I

snorkel for sea glass, but it's great exercise. I like the western beaches. It's easy to get in and out compared to the rest of the sea and their reefs—I spend an hour doing that. I soak up the sun for a bit, and it's lunchtime by the time I get home, shower, and make myself something to eat. Then it's playing piano, crafts, working on something regarding the apartments I own. It's probably dreary compared to your life."

"Not at all. It sounds normal and balanced."

"What about your days?"

"I work six hours a day, five days a week, from my home. I am semi-retired, hoping to retire within the year or so."

"What kind of work?"

"Security. I shall explain down the road, but when people ask me what I do, I tell them import-export. I will not lie to you, Joz—I promise to tell you more after you know and trust me."

Oh, boy. "Nothing illegal, I hope…"

Frank laughed. "Quite the opposite. One day I shall share more—"

I wish you'd share now.

"—and my day off is Saturday. Shall we sail and enjoy the water?"

"I've never sailed and wouldn't know how to help, but I would love to go."

"I shall handle the sailing. You enjoy the sun, breeze, and salt spray."

"May I bring something?"

"A swimsuit. We may stop and dive into a lagoon to cool off. I will stock everything we need. How about ten in the morning?"

"That sounds great."

"Very well." He kissed her, pushed off the bed, and stood. "I must get you back to your car and get on to work." He pulled a card from his wallet. "Text me your address; I will collect you Saturday morning for our first real date."

Chapter Seven

After a thrilling sail on a typical island day filled with sunshine, Joz turned into a believer in non-motorized sea travel. Likewise, Frank began meeting her for snorkeling once a week before he went to work, pointing out octopus' holes and reefs filled with fish and eel. With her boyfriend at her side—Is that what he is? She felt safe swimming farther out than usual and sometimes swimming with sea turtles and dolphins.

A month later, after a Saturday dinner with Joz at the Salty Pond sans pepper, he suggested a walk on the beach before sunset.

"Let's toss our shoes in the car," he added.

"Whatever you think," Joz said, doing the same thing. He rolled up the cuffs of his khakis before they took the ground-level boardwalk to the beach, strolling hand-in-hand under a rising moon while enjoying the sounds of the surf on a high tide.

"Jozelyn, we are perfect together," he said. "Your sweetness, agreeable nature, and your appreciation of nature suits me. We enjoy similar things, and we like one another—very much. Please consider moving in with me."

Oh! I heard that right, didn't I?

"If you think I'm moving too fast for you, I understand, but at almost sixty-five time isn't exactly on my side. I shall be your champion, your benefactor, your protector." He squeezed her hand. "Call me your forever love. And you won't lift a thing, darling. My men will move everything from your house. Stay with me."

"Frank," she said carefully, "I've been on my own for some time—"

"Damnation!"

Joz's heart sank. That was an unexpected response. The last thing she wanted to do was hurt him, her heart torn between a quick yes and a careful consideration. She stopped their stroll and turned to him. "Please understand that I'm not saying—why are you standing on one leg? What's wrong?"

"Cactus," he grunted. "I stepped on a thorn … or two."

"Well, sit down. I'll pull it out for you. I prefer the west-end beaches—no cactus in their sand." This, for the moment, would delay the choice she would have to make, but only briefly. His request wouldn't vanish into the ether; it would hang over them like the ultimate elephant in the room until she said either yes or no. Frank lowered himself carefully to the sand. Then he gasped.

"Bollocks! Damnation! Hellfire!" he muttered.

"Now what?"

"More cactus … in my private areas, too."

His face, she saw, was a brilliant shade of crimson. She knew not to smile (and absolutely wouldn't laugh at his plight), but now she didn't feel quite so backed into a corner.

"Well, I'll be glad to pull those out," she purred, checking the sand before she kneeled to help.

"I'm afraid you might find a whole field of them."

The thorns in his foot came out quickly. Frank

pushed carefully back to his feet and was able to stand, but it was clear he wouldn't be able to walk comfortably without assistance. Joz could see him trying to hide his discomfort, but he looked to be in intense pain.

"Let's move closer to the water where we'll be free of cactus attacks," she said, taking his arm. He nodded and managed to shuffle several feet from the patches of sea oats that had camouflaged the cacti hell.

"Okay, this will do. Now, put your derriere toward the sun before it sets—oh, dear. It's like you sat on a porcupine. I'll start with the ones that stick out through your pants."

"Hurry or I may lose my manly bravado."

"At least you haven't lost your humor, and losing your manly bravado would be impossible," Joz said. She counted five thorns she pulled out with cactus flesh on them. "Do you feel this?" She gave his backside a light rub while feeling for more thorns.

"Hold your horses, my sadistic woman." Frank sidestepped her. "They attached themselves. You mustn't tap them in deeper."

"Then you'll need to drop your drawers for me to see."

"If I must." Frank undid his khakis and dropped them.

Joz blinked when she realized he was going commando. "Your body amazes me. How do you keep such tight muscles?"

"That's the way—Ouch! Sweet-talk me through the pain."

"I love this wonderful view."

"Good God, I love a temptress, but your timing—" he said through gritted teeth.

"There, I got them all. Shall I kiss your cheeks to make it better?"

"Why didn't I meet you earlier in life, woman?" Frank moved to take her on the deserted public beach.

"I don't know about this—we don't want any more stickers."

"All right, my love, we shall save it until you move in."

Joz looked up. "I haven't said yes… yet… and we have company. You better cover up."

His smile absolutely slayed her as he made himself presentable. Once again, he took her hand, and they nodded at the couple coming toward them.

"Now that you pulled out thorns from this old man's rear," he said once the couple was out of earshot, "you have officially experienced the worst of me. Please say you will live with me."

So much for the elephant in the room—they would deal with this right freaking now. She took a deep breath, trying to collect her thoughts. Part of her wanted to jump into his arms. Part of her wondered if this was a bad idea.

"If you promise to stay the Frank that I've come to love without changing into another person afterward, yes, I'll move in with you."

He brought her hands to his lips and kissed them. "Oh, that is an easy promise to make. Let's start tonight—come home with me."

"Well, it's about time. I should at least see your house before moving into it."

"I had avoided sharing my private space for professional reasons. But the time has come, Jozelyn. My home is a part of me, of who I am." He slipped his arm around her, as they walked to the jeep. "Besides, I do hope you might volunteer to spread antiseptic on my wounded derriere."

"Of course, especially since I've seen all the damage."

"Oh? More than from thorn wounds?"

"Yes. I saw a huge crack."

Frank burst into laughter. "Lover, nurse, and comedian. That is quite an attractive combination."

Chapter Eight

Frank headed toward home, moving away from the mix of natural fauna and high-end condominiums that dotted the eastern-shore roads and made a sharp left.

"I don't recognize this…" She peered out the window.

"It's my driveway."

Joz, her mouth falling open, watched as he wound up a thousand-foot mountain lane. "I like living on top, keeping an eye out for anyone coming and going. I prefer the safety it affords."

"Safety?" She turned to him. "It's time you spill, Frank—I mean it. Your work sounds dangerous. What is it, exactly, that you do?"

Frank didn't take his eyes from the road. "High-risk undercover work for the government."

"Which government? England or the U.S.?"

"England, although I also have helped your boys out on occasion."

"You mean like a detective, or C.I.A. work?"

"If I tell you, I shall have to kill you."

Joz chuckled but looked worried at the same time.

Frank turned and patted her knee. "Pulling your leg, love. Teasing, I admit, is not a smart way to earn trust."

Relieved, she watched as a stone cottage came into view at the top of the drive. Flamboyant trees with showy red flowers filled the yard. Allamanda, Bougainville, and fruit trees lined a walkway to the house. The immaculately landscaped area left her speechless until Frank parked and came around to open her door.

"Welcome to our home, Jozelyn."

The sun dropping in the western sky blended vibrant oranges, pinks, and yellows while competing with a surprisingly bright full moon on the rise.

"This is magnificent," she murmured. "It's like a scene from a movie, or a fairytale. So beautiful—like visual poetry created by God."

"I was hoping you might like it," Frank said. "How about an evening of stargazing poolside, and then we go where the night leads us?"

Joz caressed his arm. "You know where it will lead us."

****

The next morning Joz used Frank's toothpaste, clipped her hair into place, threw on her dress, and searched for her shoes. They'd made love on a double-wide float in the pool before cuddling and watching the stars as the water lapped softly beneath them. She barely remembered them showering outside and coming into the house and upstairs to bed.

"Frank?" she called out. "Frank, are you home?"

Walking into the living room, she spotted a note on a credenza with her name on it. Panic shot through her—was he having second thoughts about her moving in after all? Before she could reach the note, there was a tapping at the front door followed by a doorbell. She took two hesitant steps and paused. "Who is it, please?"

"Florist, madame. Delivery from Frank Loveland."

Relieved, Joz opened the door to a smiling islander

holding two dozen yellow roses with a card. It read FOR MY LOVE.

"Oh, my… I must find a tip," she said to the man.

"I've received Mr. Loveland's generosity already. Enjoy your day."

She closed the door behind him and felt mist in her eyes at the sight of the beautiful yellow roses as well as the emotional rollercoaster she'd taken then. Striding to the credenza, she tore open the envelope and read the note:

I'VE TAKEN THE LIBERTY OF USING YOUR HOUSE KEYS. MY EMPLOYEES ARE PACKING YOUR THINGS—PLAN FOR THEIR ARRIVAL WITHIN HOURS. I LOOK FORWARD TO OUR LIVES TOGETHER. LOVE, FRANK.

Joz, about to go search for a vase, stood still and tried to process what she'd just read. This man she'd known only a month (but had fallen deeply in love with) had taken it upon himself to have his staff enter her home, pack her things, and move them here? The nerve, the presumptuousness… it was jaw-dropping. She imagined her friends as she'd last seen them, Cammy and Grace and everyone as the sun set on Amelia Island, Jemma releasing sage into the air, and imagined trying to explain what a wonderful, loving man Frank Loveland was, and, well, she trusted him. The girls would have hooted and hollered, but Joz could see Cammy talking seriously of an intervention.

She marched into the kitchen and opened several cabinet doors before spotting a plain glass vase that would show off Frank's lovely gift. Placing the bouquet inside and watering them, she stepped back from the vase, admiring it, and saw herself face to face with

Cammy.

Frank loves me. He's kind, he's caring, and he listens. Give me some credit, Cammy—you above all others have encouraged me to do for myself. And I have. I've found the man of my dreams. He demonstrated his commitment to me by having my things moved here.

Having won the debate, she took a closer look at the interior of the home—she would be living here. The vaulted ceilings seemed especially steep, almost like the art gallery. Paintings adorned the walls, of course; that was the art lover in Frank. A pair of magnificent sculptures balanced the room's heavy leather furniture, and her favorite sculpture from their night at the gallery sat on its pedestal in the corner. The painting of waves crashing against a house on fire was riveting—she felt herself staring at it but had to pull her eyes away as her head began to hurt.

She moved outside to the far end of the pool's deck and faced the ocean breathing the salty air that eased the pain. Looking down, she realized she was three stories up. Frank had described his home as a cottage, but it was quite large, hiding its dimensions below on the mountainside.

"It's a freaking estate sitting on a mountain, with incredible views," Joz muttered to herself, returning to the living room. "And I live in it with the love of my life."

As if in response, Frank opened the front door then and stepped into view. Joz froze—it felt like she'd been caught. Then a bolt of love surged through her, and she trotted forward and jumped into his arms, kissing him passionately on the lips.

"Ah, the florist made his delivery on time," he said.

"I don't remember mentioning that I love yellow roses. Thank you. They're beautiful."

"My pleasure. Have you eaten?"

"I'm embarrassed to say that I just got out of bed and dressed. You wore me out completely."

"I certainly hope so." Frank set her down and held up a white pastry box. "How about coffee and an assortment of croissants and patisseries?"

"With orange marmalade?" she asked sweetly.

"Indeed. No protein, but we shall shop for eggs for tomorrow."

They ate poolside. Afterward, Frank suggested a loveseat inside with an ocean view.

"Joz, I believe that people who hurt intensely in their hearts possess a higher standard of integrity than the average soul," he said after taking her hand. "They feel deeply and upset easily when people throw anger or insults at them."

"I agree," she said.

"Trustworthy persons employ that kind of depth. I have learned you are one of those honorable people, Jozelyn, and I want you to know that I trust you."

"I'm glad, because I trust you, too. You've been patient with my apprehensions—I think you said patience was your middle name."

"And yours as well. I am ready to confide in you about my work. You must promise not to divulge what you are about to hear to anyone else."

Her heart beat faster. "I promise. I give you my word."

"Are you familiar with M.I.6?" he asked after a pause.

"Yes, I've heard of them, from movies and TV. I've

always assumed they are the counterpart to our C.I.A."

"Yes, a somewhat fair comparison. For decades, I worked as an operative or what you might call an agent in an organization with an elite secrecy—higher than either of the two governmental bodies you mentioned. After twenty-five years in active service, higher-ups moved me to supervisor of operations. I planned maneuvers and made certain they were carried out to the letter, quickly and precisely."

"Wow. That sounds exciting.

"As I said, I am semi-retired. These days I observe, but if a difficult situation arises that requires my expertise, I advise. I must keep abreast of all events in my office."

She pictured Sean Connery for the moment. While she felt safe and protected, his words and bearing were now a bit intimidating.

"Tell me what your work requires, exactly."

"I review the most difficult undertakings, and in this world expertise is necessary. If a mission demands finesse, I weigh in with advice and direction."

She placed her hand on his thigh. "So, you would be Mr. Phelps from the Mission Impossible movies?"

He didn't smile. "Currently, yes, but without the drama. And in my earlier years, you could have compared me to the agents who accepted the mission. But real agents are pragmatic. Unless given an extended assignment, we work quickly—then experience the results. If we fail to achieve the desired outcome, it could mean failure… or our lives."

Pausing to let this sink in, Frank turned to face her. "Perhaps I should have retired earlier, but I could not let my men down. I stay in the game to some degree but plan to withdraw from the agency soon. And since I will retire soon, you may go into my office, which is right this way…"

He helped Joz to her feet, pulled her into a tight hug, then took her hand and walked her to a wall filled with portrait paintings that looked positively ancient.

"Remember, my love, top-secret. Are you prepared?"

"I think so."

Frank lifted the toe of his shoe and pressed the baseboard. The wall turned around. Now it did feel like they were in an episode of Mission Impossible.

"Come, Joz."

They entered an office the size of a small guest bedroom. It had tile on the floors, walls, and ceilings. Screens lined the walls.

"A secret room?"

"No peeking at the images, dear. They remain top secret."

Frank showed her his clandestine lair for work and the panic room behind it in case of an intruder and gunfire.

He doesn't need to know how spooked I am at all this.

When they left the office behind him, Joz repeated the entry process flawlessly and nodded when Frank said they would practice a couple of times a week.

"I must ask, Frank, is being with you so dangerous that we'll use the panic room often?"

"If it frightens you, understand that it has not been used in the eight years I have resided here."

"That's good to know. I'm a little frightened of my ability to stay levelheaded if under attack." She smiled at him the best she could. "I've begun the next chapter of my life and it's certainly an adventurous one."

"I have faith in you, Joz. If you are alone, somehow, I believe with all my heart that you could handle it." He brushed the bangs from her eyes. "If anyone asks about my line of work, tell them I am a semi-retired businessman with European interests. Import-export of various materials for construction."

"Easy enough, and it's no one's business anyway."

Frank pulled her to him as they left the panic room and office behind. "The moment I saw you, Joz, I knew you were the woman for me."

"How could you possibly have decided that?"

"Woman, you carry yourself as though you have supported a heavy load, did it, and won the struggle."

"I'm not sure how to take that," she said, half kidding. "Do I look worn out?"

"On the contrary, you appear whole, intelligent, and able—gifts that time and patience bestow."

"Thanks, but I didn't survive gracefully. I'm far from perfect, you know."

"We all lack perfection," he said as they returned to the loveseat. He situated her on his lap. "It matters if our imperfections jibe naturally or if we must work at it. You labored for years at making things work; I shall take on any necessary changes. Tell me if anything I do irritates or offends you. And don't tiptoe about—spit it out if you have something to say."

Joz gazed at the ocean, trying to come up with anything she didn't find completely perfect about this new living arrangement, and jumped when he poked her ribs.

"Okay, I hate being tickled."

He stopped promptly. "You see? Communication works with me. And enough shoptalk, already. So, you have seen parts of your new home—I know you are already familiar with the bedroom area…"

She pressed herself against him. "Oh, that's one room I won't forget."

Chapter Nine

A daily routine became second nature for Joz and Frank as the weeks passed. After working alone in his office with no interruptions, she typically greeted him with wine and appetizers before they swam laps in the pool.

On weekends they snorkeled, taking the catamaran to a secluded cove where Joz introduced Frank to skinny-dipping. After spearfishing, they grilled their catch with a side of mixed vegetables brought on board. Neither showed signs of growing tired of their mutual love of the sea.

Slowed up for a month by ongoing asthma (which Frank blamed on the layer of Saharan dust that had blanketed the island; great for warding off hurricanes, he said), she did little other than dabble in arts and crafts as she tried to regain her strength and at least a semblance of a positive outlook. At least Frank still wanted to make love.

Then, one afternoon when she announced that she felt good, Frank came up with a suggestion. "I noticed your energy picking up this past week. How about an outing at The Salty Pond to celebrate," he asked knowing she never says no to that restaurant.

"That sounds perfect," she said. "I am feeling kind of spunky."

"Spunky? Then I shall wear my brand-new sports jacket for my beautiful lady and give her a dance or two."

"That's exciting. Dresses I ordered arrived a few days ago—I've been dying to wear one."

Leaving their bedroom to change, Joz slipped into a silk sundress, a backless golden beige. She freshened her suntanned face, adding eye makeup and lipstick. Strands of loose curls fell around her neck, but she wore the rest up, knowing the sea breeze would create havoc with a shorter style. Her earrings, made from sea glass, added an island flair, and complemented the necklace and bracelet she created. When she returned, Frank had changed from shorts and polo to slacks and a short-sleeve shirt. His deep-beige jacket went nicely with her dress.

"So," she said, giving him a big smile. "How do I look? Ravishing?"

"Hmm. Something doesn't work."

She turned toward the mirror. "You don't like the dress?"

"Quite the contrary. Such a beautiful dress requires what you call bling rather than casual baubles." He handed her an elongated box. "Try this instead."

"Oh, my. You want me to open it? What's the occasion?"

"Joz, do I really need a reason to give you a gift?"

She brushed her lips on his cheek and sat at her dressing table, her heart pounding.

"Go on, open it."

"I will. I'm trying to settle down." Taking a deep breath Joz lifted the lid to find a beautiful necklace and bracelet of sapphires and diamonds. A pair of earrings sat inside that matched. She swiftly removed her homemade pieces and tossed them on her makeup table. "These are exquisite."

"This jewelry suits you, my beautiful love," he said into her ear after helping with the clasps.

"Frank, I haven't … I mean, no one ever gave me … thank you."

"Absolutely my pleasure. I am thrilled that you love genuine gemstones."

"I'd love you if you never bought me jewels. But I happily accept the cherry on top." Helping her to her feet, Frank pulled her to the full-length mirror.

"Do we look exceptional together?" she asked.

"The beauty and the beast. You look lovely, Joz."

She turned into his body, facing him. "Your compliments make me feel self-assured. And feeling secure makes me feel incredibly grateful … and carnal." She nibbled his ear.

"Joz," he said into her neck, "are we to get undressed?"

"Not yet. I'm trying to say that I appreciate you. Let's go."

****

Joz, her heart absolutely singing as Frank drove them to dinner, felt it sink when they found the parking lot at The Salty Pond completely empty.

"Are they closed, or did we come on an off day—what day is it, anyway?"

"It is our day, Joz. They are expecting us. I made a reservation."

Frank, ever the gentleman, opened the car door for her. They strolled arm-in-arm into the restaurant, where Rudolpho greeted them.

"Goodnight, Mr. Loveland, my lady. Your table

awaits."

The two-top with a sea view, Joz noticed, allowed Frank to view everyone who pulled into the parking lot.

"Look at the centerpieces on each table," she said to him. "Using conch shells for a vase with local flowers inside is artsy. And they've hung strands of party lights. But there's no one to enjoy the changes except us. Something must be going on—maybe they're preparing for a party tomorrow?"

"Stop worrying about the restaurant, and let's drink our wine while we wait for food."

"But we haven't ordered."

"We are creatures of habit, ordering the same dish every time." He winked at her. "I told Chef to make our regulars. Is that acceptable?"

"Well, of course, it is," she said, embarrassed. I need to shut up with all these questions and just enjoy the evening. "Oh, there's Junee. He reminds me of a surfer boy, sailing enthusiast, and aspiring professor."

"Goodnight, Junee," she said to him. "The centerpieces look lovely, and the party lights add romance."

"Thank you, my lady. Goodnight, Mr. Loveland."

Junee acted positively giddy while pouring Frank's wine. Frank tasted and nodded, waiting for the server to fill both glasses before he spoke to Joz. Another smiling server peeked around the corner and caught Joz's eye. Then a hand landed on her shoulder and yanked her into the kitchen.

Okay, what's going on here? "Did you catch that, Frank?"

"Joz, my love. Attention, please." He pointed to his eyes.

"The servers are acting strangely tonight, like there's something happening in the kitchen. But I will give you my full attention," she said, smiling. Staring into Frank's eyes indeed relaxed her. She tickled his chin, giving him a sexy wink as the waiter set down a basket of warm bread.

"Oh, that smell is delightful," she said. "I better eat a piece before the wine comes in for a landing."

"Great idea. I shall join you. But… we must discuss something important."

"That sounds ominous," Joz said, tasting the warm sourdough. "Don't let me eat another bite. Move the basket to your side of the table, sweetie. Even if I get on my knees and beg, don't allow me another piece."

His smile almost brought her to her knees. "Hmm… hold that thought, my darling," he said with a wink. "Junee, please remove the basket from the table. Joz and I won't be able to restrain ourselves with it sitting within a whiff of our noses."

"Certainly, sir."

"So, you wanted to talk about something?"

She noticed the tiniest change in his body language. That, plus the weird way the staff is acting… "Joz, we've been together for—"

"Oh, God. I've forgotten an anniversary, haven't I?"

"No, Joz, and do not bury your pretty face in your hands. Look at me."

This was either going to be very good or very bad, but if something bad was afoot, he wouldn't drop it on her at a fine restaurant, would he? She felt tense—her eyes watered and her lower lip quivered as a stiff sea breeze flipped her bangs to the side.

"Joz, my love…"

"Yes?"

"Oh, for heaven's sake, Jozelyn, will you marry me?"

Time seemed to stop. Joz's scalp itched, and she wondered if she'd heard right. Her lips moved, though she couldn't tell if she'd answered him. She was dimly aware of several sets of eyes on them and the haunting scent of the sourdough, safely out of reach of her trembling fingers.

"I have been romantically trying to ask you to be my wife, to make us official, and I am quite sure I sound like an idiot. But I am asking—please say yes." Frank pushed a small box forward. "Please open it."

"You want me to marry you?" she stuttered. "A legal, binding marriage?"

"Yes. Please open the box."

"Uh… no."

He looked like he'd been slapped—somewhere between stunned and confused. He tapped his fingers on the table, like he was trying to recalibrate. "No, you won't marry me, or no, you won't open the box?"

"God knows I love you with every piece of my heart and soul …"

There was his smile. "And body. So, why the problem with saying yes?"

"Me. I'm the problem." Now she felt tears in her eyes and tried desperately to blink them back, not wanting to cause a scene. "Yes, we're two peas in a pod," she said quietly. "I don't believe a day will ever come when I won't want to touch you and love you."

"All of that is wonderful! And the problem?"

"Frank, this isn't funny at all. You break my heart in two."

"I am not following. I asked, with a ring, for you to marry me, and you say no, but I break your heart? Please explain your fear of marriage to me."

"Marriage means forever, but I'm a mess. This past month proved that to you and me—my nonstop nebulizer and breathing treatments. I'm not going to get better with age."

"Joz—"

"You may want to spread your wings after you retire, but I won't be able to—you'll be saddled with me. And I love you too dearly to do that to you."

Again, he started to interrupt. She held up her hand.

"You'll feel hemmed in by my inabilities and want to move on. Marriage makes that messy with divorce, resentments, and heartache. Without the legalities, we understand that we will be together for as long as possible. After you tire of all my physical quirks, you can end our relationship. I'll be devastated, but I will understand. It's easier than the mess of attorneys getting involved."

"Ah, I see," he said. "On this night that I ask you for your hand in marriage, you conjure thoughts of an easy breakup."

God, I've really hurt him. "No breakup comes easily," she said, trying not to squirm in her chair too openly. "I'm too tenderhearted for such things. I love us because we don't discuss tomorrow—we live from day to day. It's an honest relationship, and you stay with me because you want to be with me, not because a signed paper forces you to."

He leaned forward, his eyes dark. "Jozelyn Hardt, who the hell are you to tell me what I shall feel in the future?"

"I've been down this road before," she said weakly, using the glass of wine as a crutch. She took a sip, then another.

"Did you go down that bloody road with me?"

In her mind, Joz saw her friends back on Amelia Island. All of them, Cammy included, seemed to be staring at her as if she'd lost her mind.

"No, I didn't," she admitted, looking down.

"You project into the future and saddle me with timeworn baggage? Do you think that is fair to me?"

A fair question. At least he's lowered his voice. "Of course not. But that's what I fear."

"This is about trust, then—your lack of it in me. And that causes your hesitation? Do I worry you on a day-to-day basis? Do I make you feel insecure in any way, Joz?"

She looked up and took his hands. "No, Frank. Never."

His shoulders slumped as he exhaled quietly. "Then trust me to know my heart and mind. Trust me to love you completely, to be here for you should you become completely disabled. Have faith that my love for you is deeper than the surface bullshit you experienced in the past. Are you happy with me?"

"Happier than I've been in my entire life."

"Then, Joz, open the box. I insist that you marry me and make us officially legal." He placed his chin in his hand and covered his mouth in a way that reminded her of the comedian, Jack Benny. Then he nodded at the box. "Joz?"

Open it, Joz.

That was Cammy's voice, and Joz nodded internally. She took a deep breath, exhaled carefully, and sent her bangs fluttering, then removed the lid with fingers that barely cooperated and gasped at an enormous diamond ring surrounded by sapphires.

"It's stunning. It's absolutely the most beautiful ring I've ever seen, and it matches the jewelry you gave me earlier."

"They belonged to my great-aunt, the Duchess of Hampshire. Today, they belong to you. But wait …"

The Duchess of Hampshire? When was he going to tell me about her?

Frank was on his feet. She watched him walk to the kitchen and stick his head inside. "Everyone?" he called out. "I need you to gather around Joz and me."

He returned to the table, all smiles, the staff following behind with twinkling eyes and wide smiles.

"Frank, your aunt is a duchess?" Joz managed. "Does that make you a member of royalty?"

"That's unimportant. I want witnesses to what must be the most difficult marriage proposal ever ventured. So, I shall try another round."

As the chef and employees watched, Frank got down on one knee. Joz's heart absolutely thudded and she wondered if she would pass out.

"Will you marry me, dear Jozelyn, my wonderful love?"

"Yes, I will marry you, Frank Loveland." She wiped her eyes and gave him a conservative kiss in front of the audience. Many more kisses, she knew, would follow later when they were by themselves.

"There you have it, and with witnesses," Frank said. The relief on his face made her feel warm inside—it really was nice to feel so wanted and loved. The joyous staff applauded, and the beaming female server who peeked from the kitchen came over and hugged her. Then the chef shooed everyone back to work.

Frank slipped the ring onto Joz's finger and kissed her tenderly before taking his seat. "Let's enjoy some romantic music, Rudolpho," he said, "and open the doors, please."

Chapter Ten

"Drinks and buffet courtesy of the house to celebrate the engagement of Sir Francis Winston Loveland the Third and Madame Jozelyn Catherin Hardt," the maître 'd happily announced to a group of excited people waiting outside.

Sir? Joz, sitting frozen in place, felt overwhelmed with this tidbit, not to mention the crowd that suddenly appeared as though beamed in by a teleportation device. As guests congratulated them, her favorite love songs played in the background—it took her a minute to realize that renowned singer and songwriter Peter Maren was at the piano, singing his heart out and backed by a string quartet. She had idolized him since childhood.

"How did you become a sir?" Joz asked Frank, tearing her attention from Maren and speaking in between comments from well-wishers. "And how did you arrange this engagement celebration without me having a clue?"

"Mutual acquaintances, and the title was bestowed as a formality. Knighted by the queen for extraordinary service to her majesty or something of that nature."

"My fiancé the knight. I suppose that makes me a future Mrs. Knight?"

He smiled. "Tonight, I am merely a happy bloke who will marry the woman he wished for years ago. But another surprise awaits you." Frank motioned for a couple to step through the crowd and into view.

"Hi, Mom!"

Joz's mouth flew open. She jumped up and hugged her son Erick.

"Gosh, I've missed you, son."

"You're strangling me." Erick laughed. "I've missed you, Mom. I love you."

"I love you, baby." She turned away. "I'm overwhelmed…"

"Don't cry," Erick said, gently turning her back to face him. "Mom, you can't cry while I introduce you to my girlfriend, Alicia."

"Hello, Alicia. You must learn that our family hugs." Joz wrapped her arms around the twenty-three-year-old Chinese woman with hair that flowed down her back. Alicia accepted the hug gracefully, glowing with a movie-star appearance. "I'm thrilled to finally meet you."

"Thanks," Alicia said without the trace of an accent. "I'm glad to meet you. Erick has said so many wonderful things about you."

Erick shook Frank's hand and told him it was good to finally meet in person. Then he turned to Joz. "How could we enjoy a significant night without your only son?"

"Are you staying with us, Erick?"

"No, Mom. Sir Loveland rented a room for us at the Buccaneer Resort."

"Oh, but shouldn't we visit together?"

"Mom, this is your time." Erick gestured at her and Frank. "I'm glad you found a nice guy—he and I have had some good talks by phone. You deserve all of this, and I won't have to worry about you anymore."

****

"I'm amazed you invited my son and his girlfriend. Gosh, she's a beauty," Joz murmured as she and Frank slow-danced to a classic Maren melody. "I owe you, Sir Francis Loveland the Third. But how can I ever repay you?"

"By marrying me. Before the night ends, you shall become Mrs. Frank Loveland."

Joz tried not to laugh thinking his words were meant as a joke. Then, she saw that serious look. "Wait—what? Before the night is through? That's impossible… is it even legal?"

"I finished the paperwork. It isn't difficult if you are Sir Francis Loveland the third, my dear. Remember those papers I asked you to sign?"

She frowned in concentration, which was difficult after the generous glass of wine she'd had. "Papers. You mean when you asked me while I was in the shower a week ago? Uh, Frank, it was for the lease on the apartment."

"A tiny white lie—the only one I shall ever tell you. You signed a marriage license. We are set to go, and the minister is ready." Frank raised his finger. "If you refuse, Jozelyn Hardt, I shall sue you for breach of contract since you agreed to marry me with witnesses, no less."

She kissed his cheek. "My fiancé, the scoundrel, and trickster of the best kind. I'm almost sixty and living a fairy tale.

"Quite right. I will not give you a chance to flee or conjure an excuse of any kind." Frank twirled his fiancée by their table.

"I'm ready for my second glass of wine after this

song finishes."

"Remember, it inebriates you quickly. Better sip it." He raised his glass to hers. "To my forever bride."

Joz rested her head on Frank's shoulder and closed her eyes, savoring the moment as they continued to slow dance. This felt so right, from the man who was holding her to the overwhelmingly positive response from Erick. The icing on the cake, as she thought of it, was the first impression Alicia had made. The gorgeous young woman struck Joz as warm and genuine—

"Excuse me, may this living legend kiss the bride and enjoy a dance with her?"

Joz's eyes popped open at the query. Standing two feet away, his smile larger than life, was Peter Maren. She'd been dimly aware that the string quartet was in the middle of a classic Maren hit without hearing his piano and that legendary voice. Because he'd walked over to them. Because Peter Maren wants to dance with me. Joz felt herself blush from head to toe and wondered if she would faint. Frank gave her shoulder a squeeze as he stepped away—he was grinning like a schoolboy. Then he clapped Maren on the back in a friendly gesture before nodding to Joz.

"Shall we, my dear?" Maren asked, stepping forward to continue the slow dance. The man's British voice sounded just like it did in the thousand or more interviews she'd heard him give over the years. And to her absolute astonishment, he softly crooned the final verse of the song the string quartet was playing into her ear. She was aware of his cologne as well as a degree of physical strength, though nothing resembling Frank's presence and bearing (no surprise considering Maren was in his late seventies). When the song ended, Maren kissed her cheek, stepped back, and bowed before her. "It was a pleasure to meet you, Jozelyn," he said, a twinkle in his eye that nearly melted her. "You have found a good man. Here is to many years of good health and good cheer."

"Thank you... Sir Maren," Joz managed to say through blurry eyes. Only now did she realize that the many guests had all backed away to watch the scene unfold before them and give her and Maren room to dance. Frank approached Maren with an outstretched hand. They shook hands and embraced, and Frank said something in the superstar's ear that made him chuckle. Then Maren, with a final smile and wave at Joz, started back to his piano and received a warm ovation.

"Frank... you arranged for Sir Peter to dance with me and sing to me?"

"Yes."

"And how did you manage that?" Joz asked as Maren and the quartet went into another favorite.

"Pete and I met in Liverpool long ago. He owed me a favor."

"I suppose you'll tell me what that favor was at some point...?"

"Maybe." He winked and gave her a devilish smile.

* * * *

After five days of honeymooning at Buck Island National Park, the happy couple returned to their routine. That routine included Frank reminding the housekeeper, who came once a week, to dust thoroughly for Joz. Then he would slip into his office.

Days and months passed with sailing, snorkeling, or lounging by the pool. They read from the New York Times bestseller list, sharing space on an oversized hammock that hung in the shade between two palm trees. On rainy weekends they enjoyed movie days or strip poker.

On their six-month anniversary, Frank rented a glass-bottomed boat to cruise through the bioluminescent Salt River Bay during a full moon. The couple brought champagne and cheese onboard to celebrate as a hired captain sailed them over the waters. As they clinked their glasses together, Joz felt just as much in love with him as she did on their wedding day, if not more so.

****

The next morning, Frank submitted his request for retirement to the agency. It was time, he knew. He'd truly found his soulmate in Joz and wanted to spend every minute of the rest of his life loving her and taking care of her. The response from his superiors was quick and to the point.

They were not accepting his resignation.

Chapter Eleven

Joz, staring out a bay window and sipping lemonade on a sunny afternoon later that week, set down her glass as her thoughts returned—as they did about a hundred times a day—to Frank. His six-hour day was almost finished. She pictured them walking on the beach, then stepping into the surf, gradually at first, touching their toes in the water. They had something of an unspoken routine: a bit of swimming, a bit of playfulness, then one of them would take the other... A jolt went through her body that extended all the way to the tips of her fingers and shuddered at the thought of him inside her. She was catching her breath when her phone chimed with a text.

—*MY BRIDE. I SHALL BE WORKING THROUGH THE NIGHT ON A COMPLICATED BUSINESS VENTURE. MY MINI FRIDGE IS WELL STOCKED.*

DON'T WORRY ABOUT TEA FOR ME. SEE YOU IN THE MORNING.

YOUR FRANK.—

"Okay," Joz said, speaking aloud to her phone as if it were a live person and capable of having a conversation. Feeling abandoned and alone, she pictured Frank in front of her. "What now? I'm used to greeting you outside the office this time of day. I made appetizers like I always do. And I was counting on my hug and kiss."

She stared at the framed photo of her and Frank on the boat when they had invited another couple fishing. The photo captured so much in its simplicity—Frank was in a chair with Joz on his lap. He looked so handsome, and Joz had to admit the camera had caught her on a pretty good day. She pressed the frame to her breasts.

"I admit it, Frank. I'm absolutely lost without you," she said, choosing not to give voice to what was rumbling through her mind.

What on earth would keep him working overnight?

****

Frank paced the floor, watching his wife react on a screen inside his office. He was angry at the news he'd received from headquarters—only he had the capability to fix the problems that began twenty years ago. He had successfully hacked into Communist China's military accounts, moving their money to a Swiss account. He and an unseasoned agent funneled those funds into programs that encouraged democracy and, over time, would help overthrow the communist party if all went well.

The plans failed thanks to Frank's inexperienced agent.

"You fool," Frank had said. "You have painted a target on us. Communists are vengeful. They will hunt down the thieves—that being us—even if it takes a lifetime to do so."

Until the enemy had stumbled across his ex-partner, Nicholas, in a Hong Kong bar, Frank believed the danger had ended. But alcohol left Nicholas in a drunken stupor, and the dismissed agent apparently reminisced about the covert work he did years before. The bartender, a communist plant, listened carefully and eagerly passed that information along to a member of the communist party. By the following evening, Nicholas had disappeared. That was soon followed by demands from the communists that England immediately reverse the stolen funds—the estimated worth of which was over $20 million U.S. dollars. Now Nicholas was a trophy prisoner in a Chinese hellhole who was pleading for his life.

"They will not allow Nicholas to live, and I am also dead if they find me, even if every penny of those funds is returned," Frank muttered. "And there is no doubt that Nick, the weakling, will break. The enemy will be at my door any time."

He bent at the waist and exhaled sharply enough to rustle papers on his desk.

"I am a stupid senior in love," he muttered. "I have put my Jozelyn in danger."

He went to work, spending most of the night hacking into governmental agencies and fabricating documents. He only relaxed after plans had been made to send Joz to a location far from the islands. Inside a secret compartment in his mahogany desk, he removed a key wrapped in a small slip of paper that contained a safety-deposit box number. That box held the receipts for the stolen funds. Next, he searched his library for a suitable book, deciding on a pricey volume of sonnets by Byron. Reluctantly, he loosened the leather binding and slid the Swiss account number and key into it before resealing the cover to make it appear unblemished.

"The money will help Joz after I'm gone," he said aloud. "A fake passport and driver's license for her will arrive tomorrow by a special courier." He tapped the book. "That is it."

He closed his eyes. Until he met Joz, travel, secrets, and schemes were his life, but the thrill of it had died years before. His work had become habit more than choice, and he felt totally at peace with the decision he'd made to close that chapter of his life.

Now, that chapter was forcing him back into active service.

Chapter Twelve

"Good morning, my love," Frank said, slipping into bed before sunrise and spooning his wife.

"Mm, I missed my husband."

"Sorry. Work calls today, too, but I must enjoy a snuggle." He pulled her close, loving her soft, silky skin.

"You must be exhausted."

"I am. I need sleep." He let his head fall to the pillow, his hand on her breast. But before sleep captured him, he let his hand slip to her soft stomach. Beginning to rub in small circles, he worked his way downward.

"By God, woman, you feel lubricated. Were you playing without me?"

"No, but I did dream about you."

"Joz, I adore you." He swirled his finger as Joz moaned and felt his erection grow. "Stay on your side, as I slip inside." He entered her gently as his finger continued to delight her. She groaned with pleasure, breathing heavier. He knew she was nearing orgasm. "I love you, Joz. Never forget that I love you."

"Oh, Frank…" she managed before erupting with a delighted screech as he pressed impossibly close, penetrating deeper.

"Let's explode together, my love." He moved in a different way, breathing into her ear and telling her repeatedly that he loved her. As they climaxed together, perfectly in sync, he held Joz tightly and felt the familiar sensation of relief as her breathing steadied and her heart began to slow from its feverish pitch. He'd never in his life been with a woman who had such intense orgasms (which he'd told her, more than once), and he had a niggling fear each time they made love that one day her heart might give out from over-exertion (this, he'd never told her). If that happened, he knew his heart would break apart as well.

Twenty years ago," he said, breaking a comfortable silence, "I would have been capable of doing this all day."

"Frank, I love you so," she said, sounding like she'd just run a mile at a good clip. "I never knew sex could be this fulfilling. You make me feel so safe wrapped in your arms—these incredible muscles—Frank, what are you doing?"

"Ready for some more? It is your fault for talking to me that way."

Once more they climaxed together. This time both were so entirely spent they fell into a deep sleep that lasted until nearly noon.

****

Joz opened her eyes, feeling incredibly refreshed, and smiled over at Frank as he continued to sleep peacefully. Not wanting to disturb him, she slid carefully from bed and crept into the bathroom, closing the door. She took a quick shower, still basking in the glow of their lovemaking early this morning, and put on a sundress after toweling off. She had decided to surprise Frank with breakfast and tiptoed through the bedroom, settling into stride in the hallway as she headed to the kitchen.

Frank stepped out from behind a wall and startled

her so badly she feared for a moment she'd wet herself. She opened her mouth, but no words came out.

"Darling, I'm sorry." He laughed. "I wanted to surprise you, but not with a heart-stopping event."

"I saw you in bed." Joz held her heart, bending forward to catch her breath.

"You saw my pillows under the sheet. You were being tactful, tiptoeing, trying not to wake me. I thought you would enjoy the coffee already made."

"Promise you won't do that to me anymore."

"I promise," he said. "And the coffee is already made. I must work after a cup—and we must talk immediately. It is important."

He turned to the counter and poured two cups, Joz adding cream.

"Frank, you worked all night—"

"I will today, also. Now please sit with me. A problem has cropped up."

"You're tense," Joz said. "I can tell this isn't good."

He didn't reply, placing a cup on each end table on the balcony. They gazed at the ocean in silence as she waited for him to explain. Finally, he took her hand.

"Something dangerous and unexpected occurred. I will need your cooperation to keep us both safe and sound. Understand?"

"I need more information to understand, but I'll be discreet no matter what you tell me."

"This will take more than carefulness and secrecy, Joz. It will require play-acting and patience—a great deal of patience."

Now she felt real worry, something akin to what she felt the night of their engagement. She took a careful sip of coffee then set her cup on the end table.

"Twenty years ago, I was involved in an operation with a rookie," Frank began. "I doubted his training and insisted he was unprepared for the importance of our undertaking. But my superiors demanded we work as a team, along with qualified members. I will not divulge anything else, except that I was correct—the agent's incompetency caused the death of two team members. As the leader, I escaped detection while the fool ran for his life. He should have kept running.

"I knew the communist regime might find him—and me—and take revenge. After twenty years passed, I thought I was finally home free, but I was wrong. China wants the money returned that I drained from their weapons coffers. They have found and imprisoned the rookie who was involved. He will divulge my name, and they will pursue me doggedly, which means they will come after anyone I love… namely you."

After Frank's lead-up, a spike of fear invaded her spine. After all, he had what amounted to a safe room carved into the mountainside to live in if in danger of an attack. As if feeling her fear, he placed a comforting hand on her knee.

"To keep you safe, I've taken elaborate measures that concern us."

"But Frank, that agent must have matured. Maybe he won't tell them anything."

"Trust me, he will sing like a bird and already has to some degree—he has placed you in great danger. But my actions will mislead my enemies." Frank started to sip his coffee, then changed his mind and set the cup down.

"Go on."

"I created divorce papers dated one week after our marriage. In them, you flew to Las Vegas to legalize the breakup. I added a few hate emails between us to legitimize the fabrication. What they find online will convince the enemy that you have had nothing more to do with me."

"Whoa—wait, Frank! You mean in the eyes of the law, we're divorced?"

"It looks that way, but you and I know better. This is the difficult part."

"It becomes harder?" She grabbed a small pillow and hugged it.

"A retired agent—a dear friend in Montana and a widower—will harbor you on his ranch—"

Joz squeezed the pillow. "Montana?"

"Hear me out, please. I would not choose this if your life was not on the line. I apologize from the bottom of my heart. After all this time, I thought I would not pose a menace to your well-being. But I thought with my heart, not my brain. Being married to me places you in jeopardy, which I cannot fix with you living on the island."

"Okay," she said, breathing out the word. "Since we're in danger, I will follow anything you suggest to keep us safe. But can't I at least stay on the island—if not in our house, at least in an apartment while we look divorced?"

Frank faced her. "No. Professionals will question your proximity. You must be removed from the equation completely, and Buck will see to your safety."

"In Montana."

"Yes, in Montana."

"I see. How soon do I go?"

"You leave on tonight's flight," he said quietly.

"Tonight? Goodbye this soon? I don't have clothes,

or coats…"

"I've ordered supplies already which are being shipped to Buck's house."

Joz sat in stunned silence. She tried to picture Cammy in her mind and wondered what her friend would say to this, but the internal screen was blank—she was apparently on her own in determining how to proceed.

"Are you all right, Joz?"

She almost couldn't hold back a scornful laugh. "Oh, I'm just peachy. Other than feeling like you've kicked me in the stomach."

"Please trust me. Concoct some things in your mind that you would enjoy seeing in Montana during our separation—"

"Which will be for how long?"

Frank sighed hard. "I do not know. Weeks for sure, possibly months. All I can tell you is that I could not live with myself if the enemy uses you as a pawn, and they will. A passport and license will arrive this afternoon in your pseudo identity. I mailed your real passport and license to Buck. He will make it seem like you left the island a year ago, and that is the story you must tell anyone who asks."

"Whatever," she snapped. "Anything you say, Frank. Just so I can follow the script, why did I fly to Montana a year ago?"

"Buck visited, and you fell in love with him and took off from here."

Joz jumped to her feet and picked up her coffee mug. "You're serious, aren't you? You've made me a floozy in addition to giving me a few hours' notice that I'm being airmailed way the hell off to Montana—and the official reason is that I ran off with your friend, and we're shacking up?!?"

"I have had you two marry," he said, still facing her. "Your name is Mrs. Buck Bigelow."

"Oh, really?" She held the coffee cup in shaking hands, tempted to throw the scalding beverage and the mug itself off the balcony—if not into his face. She felt real, raw anger at this man for the first time since they'd laid eyes on each other. "I suppose you want me to act on that, too?"

"Buck is a gentleman. I assure you of that. But you will be living in his house, and he will absolutely look after you should something happen to me."

This brought Joz up short. She nearly dropped the cup before managing to set it down. Brown liquid sloshed over the sides, but she paid no attention as she slumped back into her seat. He really thinks he might die. "Do not let anything happen to you, Frank. You hear me? No one else will ever fulfill me because my heart belongs to you."

****

This was real, and Joz had gone through a wild ride of emotions: part of her wanted to ease the pain with drink, part of her wanted to slap Frank hard enough to leave a welt (while warning him not to touch her), and part of her wanted to collapse into his arms and beg him not to send her away. Her eyes welled with tears as he stood six feet away and begged her not to hate him.

"I can't hate you, Frank. I love you with all my heart," she said quietly. "And I'm more scared for your well-being than I am my own—even though the man I love is ripping me from his life like a pair of worn-out socks. But while I can't comprehend your kind of work or motives, I will make the best of this stay in the great state of Montana. Our final moments together should be spent feeling love, not hurt, and certainly not hate."

This, apparently, gave Frank encouragement to step forward and take her into his arms. "My lady. You might have been English in a former life with your stiff upper lip."

"I'll be strong until I reach Montana. You better warn Buck that I will be falling apart on his ranch. I may stay that way for some time—we haven't been apart for eighteen months."

"I already have, my love, and you will find Buck exceptionally understanding and compassionate. Now, let me get something from the office for you."

Leaving her standing there, he stepped into the office, was gone only a minute, and returned with a book of Byron's sonnets. "Keep this well-hidden when you aren't reading it," he said. "And if anything should happen to me, study this book, Joz—feel it through and through." He lifted her chin and looked into her eyes. "You must remember these instructions: stow the book on your person in case the luggage gets lost. Do not lose sight of it for a second. Promise me, Joz. It is that important."

"It's a First Edition?" she asked flatly. "Sure, Frank. I will cherish it, protect, and keep it with me always...I mean it."

"Never forget it. Finally, a brunette wig is on the top shelf in your closet—wear it to Montana. Looking beautiful is not essential, but you must wear it to match your identification papers and photo as Mandy Samuelson. Be yourself once you get to the ranch. Remember, the timeline has Joz Bigelow already there. Mandy Samuelson... understood?"

"I don't have a choice. Yes, I'll be your Mandy Samuelson."

He nodded and checked his watch. "It is one o'clock. Try on the wig, Joz, fuss with it a bit. I must get to work while you gather your essentials."

"That's it? You'll say goodbye before I leave, but now off to work?"

"A courier will deliver your documents by three—check by the front door, please. I shall be through in the office at six. Your cab arrives at six-thirty."

Joz sighed. "The quicker, the better, I guess. At least you're staying here—"

"I fly to London tonight. It will be safer there."

"London?"

"I should not tell you that either. I have become too slow for the game. But there will not be a retirement until I pull this off."

"No, it's fine. This house represents our home, our love nest. After you leave it, I'll daydream about reuniting with you here."

This made him smile, which thawed some of the ice she felt. "That's the spirit. Now, off with you—I must get to work."

"Frank?"

He stopped and turned slowly. "Yes?"

"Have you told Erick?"

"No. Tell him we are traveling on extended holiday if you must."

Joz threw up her arms, exasperated. "I'm not a trained agent like you," she growled. "This is a life-shattering moment for me, and is not easy for me like it apparently is for you. Are you sure we have no alternative?"

Frank pulled her close and kissed her forehead. "I apologize, my love. Hurting you is the last thing I ever wanted to do. But this must be done, and in exactly this way."

Chapter Thirteen

Before dressing, Joz opened her medicine pouch and lined up the bottles on the nightstand. She swallowed pills two by two, then shoved the medication bag into her traveling purse. Turning to her carry-on suitcase, she packed the toothbrush, shampoos, body wash, and perfumes. She included frameless wedding photos of her and Frank—happy times that seemed to be slipping away.

My heart feels like an out-of-control elevator plummeting to the ground.

"I am strong. I am strong. I am strong," Joz repeated like a mantra before focusing on her clothes. "Nighties, underwear, and a comfortable pair of shoes… an airport might sell boots and a coat." She turned to her jewelry and continued her monologue. "I'll wear the most valuable ones. The rest goes inside a hidden compartment in my purse. Should I take my wedding ring off? Hmm… I'll wear it on the right finger instead. And—oh, great—I own exactly one pair of designer jeans and one sleeved blouse. I guess they'll keep me warm on the plane. I'll wear my jacket around my waist. That way I can't forget it." She strode to the closet and reached for the wig. "Oh, crud! Look at this hairpiece!"

Closing her eyes again, Joz saw Cammy in her mind. *I'm doing this for Frank.* Stop being so angry, and this thing looks as natural as a short bob and wisps of bangs can be.

Joz stood still for a moment, the wig in her hand, then did something she hadn't done in years. Falling to her knees, she clutched her heart.

"You sent Frank to me, God. Please keep my husband safe… amen."

****

Frank watched his wife through the cameras and heard every word, his guilt growing unbearably heavy. "Keep Joz safe, also," he said quietly. "Woman, you have won my heart and soul, but my queen and country call."

He turned away from the cameras. As he knew from years of experience, the mindset to succeed most definitely did not include sentimentalities or a tender heart. Fortitude was the name of the game if he wanted to live.

****

Joz zipped up the suitcase and rolled it out to the front door, her purse slung across the front of her body with the Byron book, meds, and jewelry inside. Sure enough, an envelope containing a passport and driver's license lay by the door. She opened the envelope carefully and eyed her passport photo.

"Mandy Samuelson, that's me. A convincing brunette, if I do say so myself," she added. "They do excellent work."

After slipping the documents into her purse, she retrieved her phone and checked the weather in Montana.

"Well, at least it isn't snowing," she said, continuing her monologue. "October could be a lot worse there. But, geez, twenty-nine at night is hardly inviting, and sixty during the day won't continue. They get winter early in those parts."

Grimacing at the discomfort in her stomach, which reacted like an acid factory in stressful situations, she opted for a container of yogurt and moved to the bay window to see the lovely ocean view. Settling on the couch and placing the yogurt on the end table, she paged on her phone to the pictures folder. If the many photos of her and Frank together couldn't relax her, nothing could.

"Oh my God," she hissed. "They're gone."

She confirmed this with a second, careful search of her phone. Every single image of Frank had disappeared, replaced by photos of the man she assumed was Buck. Frank (without telling her, of course) had even photoshopped a wedding photo of Buck and Joz. There she was in a wedding dress with a Montana backdrop!

"At least he left all the pre-Frank photos... yes, there's Erick, Cammy and the girls, Amelia Island." Remember what you just prayed about. Don't be angry at him. He isn't exaggerating about the danger if he's gone to this extent to protect me.

Joz finished the yogurt, decided she wanted another, wolfed that one down, and eyed sandwich makings before thinking better of it and shoving the refrigerator door shut. What she most definitely didn't need was her stomach coming unglued on the plane. She paced the kitchen floor, keeping an eye on the time, and moved to the living room, where she walked a small circle repeatedly.

"Isn't Frank saying goodbye?"

Five-thirty came and went, and no Frank. Somewhere between anger and breaking down in tears, Joz dragged herself from the bay window (where she'd collapsed a few minutes before) when a horn beeped outside at precisely six o'clock.

"Damn you, Frank!" she said under her breath. "Not even a hug or kiss?"

****

Frank, pacing in his office, watched the screen. "It's better this way," he answered aloud. He waited until the taxi pulled away before venturing outside. He stood there in the driveway, taking a deep breath of the salty air, and watched the driver take the downhill curves like a pro.

Suddenly brake lights flashed. Shaking his head and allowing a smile, Frank watched as the driver carefully backed the cab up each bend it had taken seconds before. He was unable to help himself and ran for the cab as it approached. Joz, of course, jumped out before the driver had come to a stop. He yelled an angry warning but stopped when Frank held up a hand for silence. He caught Joz as she leaped into his arms and considered, for the briefest of seconds, taking her back inside and dismissing the driver. He settled for a long, deep kiss and clung to the love of his life.

"Frank, no matter what happens, no matter where you are, I love you," Joz said breathlessly. "My heart had shattered years before we met, but you glued each piece together. You taught me to love completely, unconditionally. I am grateful for you, and I will handle whatever it is you must do… I will wait for you."

"You are my heart, everything I hold dear," he said through his tears. "Remember that during the changes to come. I love you and will love you always—never doubt it. Never forget it."

"I won't, my darling."

"I shall try everything possible to make my way

home once I eliminate the danger. Have faith in me." With that, he took her arm and guided her back to the idling cab.

"Godspeed, Frank." Joz patted her chest and his. She climbed into the cab and turned to stare at him, her hand plastered to the window like that of a young child. Forcing himself not to cry, he smiled the best he could, deeply moved at the gesture. Drying his face with his hands, he watched as the cab went back down the curves. This time there were no brake lights. Then the car disappeared behind a line of palms at the bottom of the drive.

"I have healed her, only to smash both our hearts into a thousand pieces," he muttered. "Goodbye, my love."

The words were barely out of his mouth when he spotted an unmarked truck making its way up the drive. He had just enough time to steel himself by the time the truck was a few feet away and the driver lowered his window.

"Sir Loveland."

"You and your men clear every bit of female from the house. Do you understand me? No DNA, either."

"Good as done, sir."

Frank followed a team of four men inside. He detoured to the kitchen but found he had no appetite when he opened the refrigerator. Deciding on a scotch instead, he slipped into his office and watched his employees while preparing for one final mission.

****

By midnight, the technicians had finished scrubbing the house and taken all evidence of Jozelyn Hardt to an incinerator. For the first time in eighteen months, Frank climbed into bed alone, noting that the sheets and bedspread smelled fresh from the package. He missed the hint of Joz's perfume, not to mention the sweet-salty aroma left behind by lovers. Not only did his heart ache, but a mountain of self-reproach seemed to be sitting on his conscience. He couldn't ever remember feeling such guilt.

He set the alarm on his phone for a three-hour nap. Exactly three hours and fifteen minutes later, a helicopter landed on the estate and flew him to St. Thomas. From there he boarded a private jet that flew him to London. He knew the agency would recondition him for the field. This was something he had carefully avoided in his talks with Joz. Under no circumstances—none—could he describe the process to her.

At my age, and at this level of danger, there's little chance I'll survive, anyway.

Chapter Fourteen

Joz had loved traveling years before. But when studying her tickets on the flight to Atlanta, she learned it would be a grueling fifteen-hour-plus span of flights, stops, and connections to Montana's Helena airport. *I am strong. Aren't I, Cammy?*

She bought a heavy hoodie, snake-skinned boots, mini-bottles, and snacks for the plane, throwing them inside the purse, donning the hoodie just before boarding the plane to Montana. Finding her way to her seat, she stowed the carry-on beneath the seat and clutched the purse in her lap. The two people next to her, a man and woman about half her age looked inconvenienced as she stepped past them to the window seat. Looking out the window as the plane taxied down the runway for liftoff from Atlanta, Joz checked her phone once again. No call. No text. No nothing. *It's like you cleared your mind of me, Frank. And now I'm halfway to Montana and essentially a world away from you.*

Her temples pulsated, neck stiffened, and her heart felt heavy as a boulder.

****

Frank spent the night reviewing updated information on the failed case involving his former partner. He managed an hour of sleep before the agency jet touched down at Heathrow Airport, where a dark

83

SUV with tinted windows drove him directly to headquarters on the outskirts of London. The shabby three-story brick building, Frank noted, could use pressure washing, and the trim appeared partially rotted. A small sign announcing SURVEILLANCE INC. was on the wall next to the rusted metal door. He pushed an intercom button behind the sign and announced himself.

An audible click indicated that his voice was recognized. Pulling open the heavy door, he entered a smelly, grungy room with a blanket roll; a dirty cap hung from the leg of a turned-over bar stool. He hurried to the far side of the room, where he pushed a brick that slid open a portion of the wall—and revealed a dank stairway. He stepped inside, the wall closing behind him. At the top of the stairs, another door opened to a modernized second floor. A tall string-bean of a man stepped out of his office at the sound of the arrival.

"Frank, my friend. I am pleased you are here."

Frank extended his hand. "I wish I could say the same, George."

"Sorry, my friend. Retirement provided another perspective, I am sure. Come in, sit down."

"Semi-retired. You know that."

"And a bride," George said, ignoring the comment. "I have seen photos. You married a lovely woman."

"Beyond lovely, but I followed procedure. Our divorce is posted online—I recorded a one-week marriage."

"What we must do for the queen and country, eh?"

"It is not easy for me, and the agency might have a difficult time wiping Jozelyn from my mind."

George's eyes opened so much Frank almost laughed. "I have never heard you express anything like that before."

"I did not explain the process to Jozelyn. I hope she understands one day…"

"It is for their well-being and yours. Entanglements—"

"Compromise the service and the agents. Yes, I understand the reasoning."

"Then, we hope you have one final game in you."

Frank nodded and sighed. "After you prepare my brain, I shall be ready. I have maintained top physical conditioning."

"Yes, but we all slow with age. I am uncertain if we have ever utilized an agent over sixty-five in the field."

Frank leaned forward. "About that, George. I may not survive this go-around. So, let's get some things straight: I forged the divorce papers, but the agency knows full well that I remain married to Jozelyn. If I go down, I want her as my sole beneficiary." He paused, holding George's eyes. "I shan't do a damn thing until I review the signed paperwork to that effect."

"Agreed."

"All of it, George. The widow's beneficiary included."

"I have already cleared it. Whilst we meet and discuss your plans to rid us of the Chinese, Hamish will execute the paperwork." George checked his watch. "He is here and waiting. Shall we?" The two men entered a secure conference room lined with soundproof panels and thick leather chairs around a huge teak table. Frank offered his hand to the man standing before them. A pair of menacing security guards stood on either side.

"Prime Minister?"

The man shook it with a firm grip. "Sir Loveland.

Your reputation precedes you. Let's get to it—you have reviewed the dossier?"

"I have, sir."

"England cannot endure an ex-operative threatening this agency, our country, and the queen. You must stop him, Frank. He verified the past mission regarding China, which I denied, of course. But if they locate that money, they may prove that we tried to topple their communist regime twenty years ago." The Prime Minister let his words sink in. "The Chinese are driven to win, Frank. They will save face through humiliating our country overtly or covertly."

"I shall defend the queen and bury Nicholas to save the country's reputation," Frank responded promptly and confidently. "As for the money, Nicholas is clueless. I had advised that era's Prime Minister that the stolen funds remain hidden and unreachable. And so, you understand, sir, I did not memorize the numbers to the Swiss box, and I destroyed the key. The notes shall remain in that box until kingdom come."

The Prime Minister nodded, happy with the explanation as best Frank could tell. "Glad, you cleared that up, and let's now reach an understanding: you have my blessing concerning Nicholas' fate. Godspeed, Frank." Frank watched the Prime Minister turn to George. Whatever warmth he had shown Frank seemed to disappear. "I shall be waiting for a report."

George stood at attention, something previous Prime Ministers, Frank recalled, failed to make him do. George respects this one. "Yes, sir. The second we have it."

Without a word, the Prime Minister and his security detail marched from the room. George waited until he heard the outer door close before he spoke.

"Your hands are full, Frank. Any ideas about handling the commies and our snitch, Nicholas?"

"Yes, and I shall share those plans after I review the legal documents for my wife."

"Fair enough." Leading Frank back into his office, George spoke into an intercom at his desk. "Hamish, bring in Sir Loveland's paperwork."

"Right away, sir," came the crystal-clear reply. Seconds later a Scotsman swung open the door and entered, looking like a redheaded wrestler rather than an administrative assistant.

"Stand by, Hamish. Frank is a fast reader."

Frank nodded at Hamish as he took the documents, then read carefully, checking every word. Relief poured through him—Joz would indeed inherit his wealth, which would serve to prove his genuine love for her. He signed the paperwork and passed it to George, who signed as a witness.

"She must be some woman," George said. "You seem obsessed with her."

Frank finally smiled. "Love at first sight, too. Drop any ideas about her after my death, George, or I promise to haunt you for eternity."

"I give you my word as a gentleman," he said. "Besides, you mustn't be pessimistic. You always made it through before, and you shall return safe and sound this time."

"Pardon me, sir," Hamish interrupted. "I require mailing addresses for your signed copies."

Frank nodded and pulled a business card from his pocket. "Take this—he knows what to do. Send a copy to Buck Bigelow in Montana, Hamish. You have his address."

"I do, Sir Loveland."

George stood and moved toward the door. "Very good. After clearing, everything you need is inside your briefcase. We shall expect your plans in the morning."

Frank sighed. He had been at this crossroads before, but this time he felt a deep, unfamiliar sadness and immeasurable grief—it was no better than when he kissed Joz goodbye before the taxi carried her away. He knew his life was about to change forever and willed himself to be strong.

"Let's be done with it," he said firmly. He stood and strolled down the hallway to a small room where a facilitator was prepared to tear Joz from his brain. "Goodbye, Jozelyn," he murmured. "Goodbye, my love."

The facilitator nodded at him, signaling that he was ready. Frank settled into a familiar leather recliner. Diodes were swiftly attached to his head before a second man entered and injected him with a hallucinogen that would begin the process of helping him forget the love of his life. The last step was the wireless headphones which were fitted into his ear canals. The room darkened, and a screen appeared on the wall.

Frank felt his life slipping away.

****

Joz checked her phone as soon as the plane landed in Helena. Still no text from Frank. Drinking far too much on the plane, she could burst into tears if she dwelled on this awful thought so she tried to picture Buck Bigelow in her mind from the fake wedding photo. Her mind, of course, promptly began comparing him to Frank.

Chapter Fifteen

As the airport came into view, Buck thought yet again about the almost two years since he lost the love of his life to breast cancer. It was odd that one month he lost Dabney, and the next month his best friend met the woman he had described as the girl of his dreams.

Of course, Frank had no recollection of his first two wives—they'd been wiped from his memory bank. And that was something, Buck knew, would remain a secret. Mandy Samuelson aka Jozelyn Loveland was never to know.

"Dabs, if you can, make sure this wife isn't the chatty or bitchy kind," he said aloud. He routinely talked to Dabney as if she were still alive and well. "And please don't let her be anything like Frank's second wife, the damn snob. Just make this one normal."

****

Buck, at the airport gate, studied Mandy Samuelson's photo as passengers finally streamed out. She was an attractive older woman in a brunette wig and, in the picture, was in jeans, a shirt, and jacket.

"You must be Buck."

He looked up, then broke into a smile. "I am, and you must be my roommate." They stood there eyeballing each other for a moment. The swarm of travelers was forced to step around them, some muttering unkind things. Buck wasn't about to respond.

"I've been drinking since I left St. Croix, so I'm not myself," the woman admitted. "I'll be a better person tomorrow or the next day. Well, I'll still be miserable, but I'll be sober."

"I understand, Mandy. This was unexpected."

"Unexpected? Pfft," she spat. "It was the last second—the last nanosecond—when he told me. Anyway, please carry my bag to your car. Carrying myself is a challenge. If you don't mind, I'll hold on to your arm." The last thing Buck wanted was drama, but if the woman before him felt anything about Frank like he professed to feel about her, Buck had no doubt she was hurting. They made it to his Hummer before she bent at the waist.

"I don't feel so good—"

Buck caught her before she fell. A passing security guard offered to call for emergency personnel, but Buck waved him off, assuring the man his wife had too much to drink on the plane and would be fine.

****

Joz awakened to a bumpy ride and muttered curses from her driver about the rutted state he had let the drive become. Buck cut the engine, hopped out, and opened the door nearest her head.

"Okay, young lady. We're home."

She felt a blast of chilly air, and then Buck was unbuckling her. Gently taking her shoulders, he eased her back and out of the vehicle and slowly to her feet. She'd no sooner tried to stand on her own than a fierce wave of nausea rippled through her. Buck grabbed her and helped her to her knees, where she vomited in the grass.

"Frank sure knew what he was talking about. You don't drink well, do you?"

She ignored the remark. "I need a bed for a day... and a toilet..." She retched again, continuing to dry-heave long after there was nothing left to purge. Now tears were streaming down her face. "I'm too mature for this foolishness—"

"No need to apologize, Joz," Buck said softly, his hand on her back.

"Aren't you supposed to call me Mandy?"

"I was at the airport, yes. Be yourself here. Let's go, Jozelyn."

Buck effortlessly carried her limp body into the house, through his guest room, and into the bathroom—just in the nick of time.

"I don't understand," she whined while hugging the toilet. "What's so important that Frank had to leave with less than a day's warning and send me here of all places? He knows it takes me time to adjust to change."

"He told me that, too, about you and change." Joz heard him rummaging around in the bathroom and smiled weakly when he wrung out a cold wash cloth and handed it to her. "I'll make you tea and toast and set it on your nightstand."

"There's no way I'll keep anything down right now—"

"It will be there when you can."

"Great, I'm sweating like a hog," she muttered. "A cold sweat." After a final dry heave, she began removing her clothes, forgetting that Buck was standing right there. "I'm going to get a shower. God, my stomach..."

"I'll bring in your things. They'll be on the bed when you finish," Buck said, already on his way out. "There

are plenty of fresh towels. Get some rest, Joz."
    "God, I promise, I'll never drink again."

Chapter Sixteen

Buck, sitting in a comfortable chair near the fireplace, rechecked the time and smiled at the dogs that lay by his feet. He was concerned about Jozelyn, though. She'd slept all afternoon yesterday, through the night, and was still snoring softly as he checked on her at noon. Finally, just before one o'clock, he heard stirring upstairs. A few minutes later she emerged, showered, and dressed.

"Good afternoon, sunshine," he said brightly.

"That's what Frank called me, and I hope it will be, Buck. I apologize for causing so much trouble yesterday. It won't happen again, but please don't expect much from me for a while."

"I've seen a lot worse, so don't give it a second thought. You must be hungrier than a bear in the springtime."

"Something light would be fine. It'll take some time to recover from so much self-abuse."

"Then how about tea, and what about some lunch?"

"Don't go out of your way. I'll cook and take care of my own needs."

This brought him to his feet. "Whoa—Frank forgot to tell you one important rule about living in my house: the kitchen belongs to me. I cook, and both my office and my kitchen are off-limits. Don't misunderstand... you have free run of the rest of the house and the grounds. But stay out of the kitchen, please."

"Happily," Joz said with a shrug he couldn't read. "Do you mind if I wait for my tea outside?"

"Of course not. Wrap yourself in that throw and sit on the porch. The fresh air will help—put some color in your cheeks."

She frowned. "Do I look sick?"

"You're as white as a polar bear in a snowstorm."

"Ha. I haven't heard that one since I was a kid. I'm going outside."

A chill cut through Joz as she stepped out to the wooden porch. She wrapped the plaid blanket around her, thinking that the sky seemed closer than in the islands.

If I stretch upward, I could pull away a piece of cloud like cotton candy.

The faraway hills faded into mountain peaks beyond. At least the view was comforting, and Joz mustered enough curiosity to follow a well-worn path and head toward the barn.

"He didn't warn me to stay clear of it," she muttered. "What's with him and the kitchen?"

The crisp air invigorated her, and she easily managed the barn door, which opened with a squawk. Then she sneezed loudly enough to wake the dead, she feared. The scent of fresh hay, though, brought back good childhood memories of jumping from the loft into hay piles and sledding down the steep hill, which had been built for hauling farm equipment that brought hay to the second floor.

Buck's barn, she noticed, was one story but had a high-sloping ceiling. It contained six stalls, all empty save for one that held sacks of feed and hay. Straw and hay bales filled the loft above. Beyond the open door on the opposite end of the barn, she saw a corral with two horses and two donkeys. They seemed content to soak up the sunshine. Thinking the blanket might scare the animals, she decided on wearing her sweatshirt later to visit them. She shut the barn door, turned, and saw two dogs sprinting toward her, barking, and baring their teeth. This frightened her, but she held firm.

"Easy does it, sweethearts," she said gently, her voice higher pitched. "I'm a guest, nice doggies. Let's go to the house. Come on."

She walked toward Buck's log home at a leisurely pace and was almost there when she heard a whistle. The dogs, which were several steps behind trying to sniff the stranger, forgot all about her and sprinted toward the house.

"Ready for lunch and tea?" Buck called out.

"Yes," she said, picking up her pace. "Your Aussies startled me after I startled them," she said when she reached the porch. "Tell me their names."

"They were Dabney's. The boy with two blue eyes is James. The one blue-eyed boy is Bond." Joz giggled for the first time since leaving Frank. "How clever!"

"My wife had a sense of humor—shy but a smart gal. She would have respected you for not running from the dogs."

"My dad taught me to carry a big stick in the fields and not run from animals unless it's a bull. I knew someone who ran from a bull."

"Did he live?" Buck asked with a grin.

"After he jumped a six-foot fence. That vision will live in my brain forever. Townies in the country—funny at the time."

"A townie, huh? I would have bet on the bull that day."

Buck didn't force a lot of conversation as they ate, which Joz appreciated, and the bread and omelet were tasty. She found the tea delicious.

"It's Dabney's blend and should be good for your stomach. I bake whole-grain bread like this, but don't expect cakes or pies—I cook and bake healthy. The eggs come from my chickens. Their coop sits on the other side of the barn." He stood and gathered the dishes. "I'll show you 'round tomorrow. You lay low today, get your strength back."

"I won't fight you on that—I feel like a flat tire. If you don't mind, I'd like to enjoy some more fresh air and say hello to the horses."

"Sure. You'll be safe, but stay far from the stallion—the black one, he's mine. Black is his name, and he doesn't care for anyone except me."

"All right. Do you have carrots or apples?"

"I'll get them. But make sure to throw the one to Black." He went inside for the snacks and was gone for less than a minute, returning with apples in a paper bag as well as a beautiful leather coat. "Here you go—horse treats, and a winter coat from Frank. He must have paid in gold for a delivery this fast."

Joz's heart soared. She tried it on, mumbling that she hadn't worn a leather coat in years, and was thrilled that it fit perfectly. The gift lifted her spirits and quashed, for now, her growing fear that Frank had abandoned her for good.

"Thank you, Buck. I feel better. And if you want to talk about Dabney, I'm a good listener, despite the impression I've probably given you. I'd love to hear whatever you'd be comfortable sharing about your lives together."

He looked past her into the distance. "She was the best of the best. Yeah, Joz, one day I'll tell you about meeting Dabney twice: initially in England, her birthplace. You'll be going through withdrawal yourself—which will feel like slides into hell with occasional lifts into purgatory—but you'll level out eventually. Maybe, sometime down the road, we'll share stories."

"Sounds like a plan." She started for the barn with the paper bag in hand.

Down the road? How long does he think I'll be in Montana?

Chapter Seventeen

The horses and donkeys watched Joz walk toward them. They became more excited with each step, recognizing the bag she carried. One by one, they came toward her—except for Black. His ears lay flat, and his eyes glared while nostrils flared. He pawed the ground repeatedly, kicking up dust that a breeze carried off toward the house.

"Don't worry, Black. I'm not going to steal your ladies. I brought a juicy apple for each of you." Joz kept her voice sweet and low, oohing and cooing with the big stallion standing on the other side of the paddock.

Black snorted as the donkeys and mare lined up instead of swarming. "I bet Dabney trained you to wait in an orderly fashion."

Each animal took an apple, the donkeys as if doing Joz a favor, but the horse nuzzled her face and enjoyed a pet before taking one.

"Aren't you sweet? I'm so glad you trust me. I hope you'll be my friend, pretty lady." She turned to the stallion. "Okay, Black, I get that you don't trust me yet." Joz kept her distance but aimed, throwing the apple on the ground in front of Black. She'd turned to walk to the barn when she saw Buck sprinting toward her and waving his arms.

"No, Black, no!"

She felt the presence of the big horse behind her the instant before a blinding pain shot through her shoulder. Then she was slammed to the ground.

"Go, Black!" Buck shouted, clapping his hands at the angry stallion. Joz, daring to look up, saw the horse raise its tail and trot indignantly away. Buck grabbed her hand and pulled, which hurt like the devil, but she saw what he wanted and was able to twist her body so she could slip under the hand-hewn rails. "Feed the horses from outside the fence," Buck muttered angrily.

"Now you tell me."

"My fault for assuming you'd know that. Let's get you in the house. We'll examine the damage."

"It hurts but not badly. I'm more surprised than anything else."

"He bit you. Your body may be in shock, but you'll feel pain once it wears off. Look, Black left his imprint on your coat—that's how hard he bit you."

Her heart hurt at the possibility of Frank's lovely gift being ruined. "I hope he didn't tear it."

"Doesn't look like it. Come in." He helped her to her feet and offered an arm to guide her. He led her inside the house and to the kitchen, asking her to sit at the table and get rid of the coat and her top. He became impatient when she tried to manage her layers of clothing to bare her shoulders.

"Joz, we're adults, pull them off."

"Modesty isn't the problem. My shoulder and back are throbbing."

"Black probably hit your shoulder blade. I'll help by taking off the easy side. Then I'll pull it over the damaged shoulder."

Working carefully around the injury, Buck gently

pulled her clothes until she sat in jeans and a bra. He grimaced at an oval bruise of red and purple.

"Okay," he said. "Black's teeth got to your skin but didn't break it. That's good. But I'm concerned about your shoulder blade. That area is swelling."

He reached into a cabinet and grabbed supplies without a word. Joz watched him pour alcohol on a cotton ball, swabbing the injury while she thought about how a man she hardly knew was touching her.

This is Frank's closest friend. Trust him until you have a reason not to.

"Tender?"

"Yes, it hurts—you were right."

"Joz, if I hadn't looked out the window, you'd be in a lot worse shape. Possibly dead."

She jumped when his probing fingers hit an especially tender area. "Why keep such a dangerous horse?"

"Stud service," Buck said promptly. "And he's only dangerous with strangers. He's fine with me."

"Well, aren't you the lucky one?"

He ignored the sarcasm. "Let's check the shoulder to make sure nothing is broken. I'll maneuver it for you."

"You have—ow!—medical training?"

"Yes. The good news is no breaks, but the bone could be chipped or cracked. We'll have to counteract the swelling and bruising. We'll keep it iced and give your body a chance to heal."

"Okay, Frank—" She felt humiliated and knew her face had gone red. She lowered her head, which made the shoulder injury hurt even worse. "—I mean Buck. My apologies. I'm sure that won't be the last time."

The flood of tears came suddenly. She wasn't sure if it was the physical pain or the reminder yet again that Frank was gone from her life at least for a while, and maybe forever. She managed to cover her face with her hands and tried to catch her breath, but it was difficult. She heard Buck scamper away—he moved fast for an older man—and returned in seconds with her inhaler.

"Easy. Breathe in."

"Here I am angry at Frank, a man who has been nothing but wonderful to me. My life went from perfect to utter chaos in a matter of hours."

"That, my dear, *is* life. Broken hearts hurt no matter their age," he said, helping her from the chair. He walked to a large couch in a dimly lit living room. A fire crackled in a floor-to-ceiling fireplace made of river rock. He poured a shot of whiskey and handed it to her. "Drink it down. I can tell you from personal experience that it works for bouts of hysteria. And grief."

She did, and felt the warmth inside her. She sat still and closed her eyes, calming down after several minutes of comfortable silence. Buck sat next to her but a respectful four feet away.

"You mentioned grief," she said. "Is that what I'm going through?"

"Sure. No one must die to feel grief. You grieve the loss of a perfect life, a perfect relationship. It's no different."

Joz shook her head. "You earned the right to mourn because your Dabney died. But my Frank lives—we're just separated. I've no business putting you through this."

Buck reached over and took her hand. "Joz, I'm a pitiful lost puppy—I needed this. Dabney died two years ago, and I've gone through the tears and the drunken weeks and months. I couldn't be the best man at your wedding, but life exists after death and after grief. I'm over the hump of it, finally, and I'm glad Frank called because you've given me purpose. I couldn't help my wife, but I can and will help you—please let me without feeling guilty about it. Deal?"

Joz nodded. Her nose was running uncontrollably and Buck, who seemed to anticipate everything, produced a clean white handkerchief and handed it to her.

"Another shot?" he asked.

"No thanks." She waved the idea away. "That one worked well enough."

"You won't be wearing pullovers for a week."

"I have exactly one warm shirt, Buck."

"Well, then, I have good news: special deliveries came while you slept yesterday. Boxes of warm clothes, I suspect. I'll bring them into the den; we'll pretend it's Christmas morning and check out what Frank sent. But, right now, we better get you into something warm."

He returned with a flannel shirt that he buttoned for her and rolled up the sleeves. She smiled and said she could wear it as a midi dress. He maneuvered the couch to recline and placed an ice pack on her shoulder, then helped her put up her feet. She felt herself relax further as she sank into the deep-brown suede built for a man Buck's size.

"That's nice and comfortable, thank you. I'm feeling sleepy."

"Yeah, my whiskey is made for a man, Joz—one hundred proof. But like I said, you took a hard hit." Then he moved to an overstuffed chair by the fireplace.

"Funny, Frank didn't mention you're an American. I thought you'd be English like him."

This made Buck snicker. "He teased me about being a colonist at Oxford, and since. I earned a Rhodes Scholarship—that's how I met Frank. We were different as a mule from a coyote, but we became fast friends. Studied together, fenced together, graduated together."

Joz was hazy now, and it took her a second. "Wait… I remember seeing swords hanging in his office."

"He allowed you into his office?"

"Please don't report him or whatever his boss requires. I let that slip after I promised not to say a word."

"It's okay. Dabney came into my office anytime she wanted. She was the soul of discretion."

"But I thought you were completely retired?"

"I am now. Once Dabney got sick, I announced my retirement from the company based in Montana. She needed me twenty-four hours a day."

"Do you ever use your office?"

"Do I keep track of operations, like Frank's?"

"Yes, that's what I'm asking. I'm worried about him."

"I use it to touch base with friends, but I'm not privy to Frank's operations, Joz. Remember, I left that agency many years before I returned to the States. I'm in the dark like you when it comes to Frank."

Do I believe that? I suppose I do… until I have a reason not to.

"I will share that of all the agents in the service, Frank was the most thorough and most cautious with details. I wouldn't worry about his well-being. Now, little lady, it's about time to close your eyes and rest."

Little lady—pfft.

Chapter Eighteen

Frank exited the clearing room, unburdened, remembering nothing of his life except his training and agency personnel. And Buck, of course, his close friend. He studied the current dossier on Nicholas, realizing that the former agent must have divulged information through the threat of torture. Trying to think along with his captured ex-partner, Frank could imagine Nicholas guessing that Frank himself would plan to hide the stolen money before the operation failed. Nicholas, if he knew his life was in danger, certainly would have shared that theory with the Chinese.

"I cannot allow the communists any information," Frank muttered as he adjusted his tie in front of the mirror. "I have retirement coming."

He met George in the same room where he'd talked briefly with the Prime Minister.

"Well, Frank, tell me your plans." George nodded for him to sit.

"In general, you shall contact the Chinese, letting them know the location of the money—decoy information, decoy money. A thief will steal the cash and leave the enemy a trail of breadcrumbs. On a boat that ends up bursting into flames, the money will burn up, the thief killed. The communists will have no recourse but to drop their objective."

George smiled. "That sounds simplistic. I expected one of your complicated scenarios."

"Complexities exist, so listen: the agency shall provide counterfeit money. I am the agent who stole it in the first place, unbeknownst to England. You shall agree to terminate my life. In exchange, the Chinese will forget the incident ever happened."

"Go on."

"A meeting with the Chinese ambassador and Prime Minister will earn the communists' trust. At that time, the agency will leak information about my whereabouts. And with both sides chasing me, I shall be swimming with the fish, dead, and the money burned in view of them. Also, the Chinese will eliminate Nicholas after they find his message to me, wanting to keep the money and split it—that, George, I will agree to."

"A-ha! Involving the Prime Minister is brilliant, as is letting the Chinese eliminate Nicholas."

"Yes, make certain the Prime Minister seems incredibly embarrassed—and thrilled that I'm dead."

George stood, as did Frank. "Certainly. We shall start the negotiations, then. Things will move quickly, so make ready."

"Sometimes, the simplest plan is the most effective."

Chapter Nineteen

Three weeks passed before Joz's shoulder felt normal. With the bruise fading, mobility returned with only a tinge of pain thanks to Buck. He'd placed her shoulder in a sling and supplied her with paperback best-sellers and on-demand movies to pass the time. They also took walks, beginning with a half hour, and each day he added ten minutes to her pitiful endurance level.

"Walking muscles aren't swimming muscles," she muttered one afternoon, clutching her aching back.

"Frank didn't give me enough notice to install a pool, but that's fixable."

Is he being facetious or serious?

"There's a hot spring half an hour away. Swim in the middle of a blizzard if you want."

"That actually sounds nice." Except for the blizzard part. "Is it deep enough that my legs will hang without touching the bottom? It's important to stretch out my spine."

"Yup, plenty deep."

"I can't wait. And I hope the new swimsuit fits. I didn't think of bringing mine to Montana."

"Why not? We have everything here that you had in the islands."

"You're funny, Buck. Last time I checked, you have no beaches."

"You've heard of Glacier Lake and Iceberg Lake, correct? Montana has its share of shorelines. They may not be smooth and sandy like your beaches, but you might find a fossil or two. Dabney's collection is in the den. Go look."

Sure enough, an assortment of fossils lined the inside of a glass case on legs.

"Oh, Buck! Dabney labeled every one of these?"

"I labeled them," he said, standing next to her. "She acted like an excited kid if she found one—we'd come home and research it together. I identified them so she wouldn't forget the scientific name and era."

"Wait—this one is a shell, a seashell. How is that possible?"

"You've heard of the biblical flood? Every culture around the world has a version of the great flood story. Did it happen like in our bible? Possibly… fossilized shells exist across our country."

"I believe in the flood. But finding ocean fossils inland? I can't wait to go."

"We'll go tomorrow, but bundle up—I'm surprised it hasn't snowed yet. Late spring and summer provide the greatest times for fossil hunting, but you'll be able to see the shoreline, and we'll give it a try. Then we'll take a dip afterward to ease arthritis. If you want, we'll grab a bite to eat while we're out. The only concern I have is your shoulder—you think it has healed enough to handle reins?"

"Yes—I won't be near Black, will I?"

"He'll ignore you if I'm on him," Buck said reassuringly.

The next day was overcast and chilly. Buck offered his arm as they walked out to the barn. "We'll take a short trail ride so you won't be hurting when we swim."

"Riding won't bother me. It'll be the getting on and off the horse that does the damage."

"Then I'll give you a leg up to make it easy on you." Buck swung open the door. "James! Bond!" he called out. "Bring in the horses."

Joz watched, transfixed, as the shepherds took off from their crouch, jumping in between the paddock rails to encircle the horses and donkeys. James headbutted the donkeys, who gave swift hind kicks before obeying. Bond drove the mare with minimal direction, but Black refused to move—he snorted and pawed the ground. What worried Joz the most was the big horse's ears that lay flat.

"Joz," Buck said calmly, "stay outside the barn until Black enters his stall. You'll ride Dabney's horse, Diana. And don't worry—I promise Black won't be aware of you."

"Even when I'm on Diana? He won't try to bite me then?"

"Not if he knows what's good for him." Buck whistled sharply. Black lifted his head and cocked one ear forward. "Let's go, Black."

Black reared, neighing before taking off toward the barn and trotting into his stall.

"That's my boy! Good job, Black." Buck handed him a sugar cube. "Come on in, Joz—have you saddled a horse?"

"That and a bridle, but it's been ages." She frowned at how old the saddle looked. "Since you don't use buckled girths, you may need to tighten mine before we go."

"That saddle's at least a half-century old. Dabney

loved the seat, so we kept it but didn't modernize. I'll tighten it after you mount, then we'll lead the horses outside. I'll take Black before you." Diana took the bit quickly, and Joz managed to stretch her arms to fit the crown piece over her ears, pulling the forelock free from the browband. She took a deep breath before she lifted the heavy saddle.

"Don't strain yourself. Wait for me to help, Joz."

"No, I'll try," she grunted. It was important to her to show this man she could pull her weight, and she inhaled deeply before swinging the saddle onto the horse. Her shoulder barked for an instant but quieted. "I'm impressed. Diana didn't budge at my clumsiness."

"She's a gentle gal. I wouldn't have let Dabney ride a temperamental horse."

"I remember the way to cinch… I think…"

"There's no need to knee Diana in the gut to make her exhale before you tighten it. Black tries me every time, hoping for a looser hold around him."

"Black is a smarty pants," Joz said, surprised that cinching the strap came easily.

"The smartest I've come across, and he could have taken a chunk of meat off your shoulder through that thick coat. But he knew it would reap some nasty punishment—as in ignoring him. You can't stand that, can you, boy?"

Joz couldn't help a smile. Maybe she was imagining things, but Black snorted and seemed to be shaking his head up and down like a human nodding yes. Buck opened the stall and led his horse toward the outside door, but Black balked as he reached Diana's stall.

"He hates me, doesn't he?"

"He needs time, that's all. He's had me all to himself

for two years." Buck tied the stallion to a fencepost. "Hold, Black," he said to the stallion. "Joz, bring Diana."

Nervously, she gathered the reins and opened the stall door to walk out her horse. Mellow Diana led effortlessly with an occasional slobbery kiss planted on Jozelyn's ear. She came up alongside Buck, giving Black plenty of space. Buck checked the girth strap for tightness.

"Good job on the cinching. Now let's get you on that saddle."

Joz bent her leg for a lift. Once she was seated in the saddle, he changed the length of the stirrups to suit her. It was then that she noticed a rifle hanging from Buck's saddle. She asked if he was expecting trouble.

"The rifle? I always plan for danger—a hungry wolf might be too brave for his own good—but that's extremely rare. We're heading northwest, so follow me until the path widens."

"I've seen too many movies that show wolves as rabid or kill-crazy. If I go out alone, I'll carry a rifle too."

"Don't believe everything you hear. Ranchers give wolves ruthless reputations," Buck said. "This was their territory before we crowded them, and they don't deserve the bad press—they haven't attacked me once. So, you learned how to shoot?"

"Frank taught me, but not from atop a horse," she said with a sigh. "He didn't plan on us being in any kind of serious trouble."

"We'll set up some bottles before long, let you take a crack at them. Gotta keep your skills sharp."

"I'd like that. I feared shooting when I began, but Frank said I would get over it. And I did."

"He was an incredible marksman. I'm glad he's

practiced all this time."

Joz's heart leapt. "You think he'll need that skill for this operation?"

Buck turned to her. "Please don't read into every word that spills from my mouth. I'm only saying it's an essential skill to keep in this crazy world."

She nodded and said nothing. He got Black moving, and Joz nudged Diana and was relieved when she settled side by side with the stallion that ignored her as promised. The trail, Joz noticed, inclined gradually upward.

"You said you met Dabney in England, right? Did she ride western there?"

"Her mother was English but married to an American," Buck said. "After her parents divorced, Dabney split time between them. She rode western in Montana but didn't ride while in England. Her mother hated horses—she hated anything her daughter loved. They were opposites."

"Interesting," Joz said.

"When Dabs spent time alone with her mother over Christmas, it drove her to the pub. She'd down a boilermaker from the stress of leaving her dad over the holiday." Buck laughed. "See, I thought she was American and said something snide about her drinking our drinks on that side of the pond. Well, she set me straight on that—said in no uncertain terms that boilermakers originated in Cornish, England. Then, she wanted to talk to me because of my Stetson and American accent. I learned that we each had family in Montana." He paused, smiling at the memory. "My dark-haired beauty, a true classic, attracted to me? Miracles never cease."

"Pfft. You know you're handsome in that rugged man's way," Joz said. "I bet you wowed the girls in London."

Buck grinned over at her. "Girl, you either need glasses or suffer from a brain tumor."

"My vision is perfectly fine, thank you. So, Dabney was a whirlwind romance?"

"Hardly. We had some great times together, but our priority in the beginning was school. Later, I was in the service of Her Majesty, along with Frank. Dabney married an Englishman, and I thought they'd live happily ever after. But—"

Joz looked up sharply when Buck paused, thinking something was in their path, but she realized he was letting the anticipation build.

"—twenty-some years later, she lost her husband and son in a horrific car crash. She came to Montana to grieve. To lick her wounds, you could say."

I know the feeling. "Please go on."

"Her father had sold their ranch many years before, so Dabney stayed at a bed and breakfast in town. We met a second time by chance. In another bar, of course. We were both close to fifty, but it was like we hadn't parted—we were comfortable, you know? I knew she endured an intense grief, a pain unlike any other. So, I invited her to stay at my ranch. Six months after that, she climbed into my bed in the middle of the night. Some months later, we married."

He sighed as they continued to climb the incline. She waited him out, sensing he wanted—maybe needed—to continue.

"I felt like I won the lottery. But it took time before Dabney returned to her bubbly self. Sometimes she'd get that faraway gaze, a signal that the grief had taken hold. I understood she couldn't forget her son and husband, and I suppose Dabs appreciated my support, but I wish she hadn't been so dang stoic. If she'd released the emotional pain—talked about it instead of keeping that English stiff upper lip—maybe the tumor wouldn't have spread like it did."

Joz blinked back mist from her eyes. "Buck, what a profound love story, if not for the excruciating end."

"Excruciating is the right word for my grief. I got through it the hard way: drinking a lot, being alone, and being angry at the world. Those things failed me. Eventually, I learned to live by being grateful."

Joz watched a hawk swoop low on the path ahead. It landed on the closest pine branch, watching them carefully as they rode. "Explain, please."

"Anytime, I'd get really low, I'd pull out my gratitude list and tell Dabney, 'Thank you for this, thank you for that.' I was lucky to find Dabs and blessed that she loved me, although our time together was far too short. But, Joz, I've had one great love in my life, while some people don't experience it at all. That's the way I survive. Gratefulness."

"A gratitude reminder. I learned that in Al-Anon, but it's easy to forget during the initial pain. Maybe thankfulness will come for me too. I'm just trusting Frank knew what he was doing with our arrangement."

"God broke the mold when he made Frank. I mean that in the nicest way possible."

Joz smiled, the comment uplifting her, and was about to respond when Black snorted and shook his head. He refused to take another step as they entered a small clearing with a thick stand of trees on three sides.

"What is it, Buck?"

"All right, boy," he said to Black. "Joz, get behind me."

Her pulse quickened when Buck pulled out the Colt rifle. He cocked his ear and listened intently as the stallion pawed the ground. Joz thought she heard twigs breaking, and it sounded like bushes were moving in two separate places.

"We're heading home," Buck said quietly. She picked up tension in his voice now. "You're in front this time."

"Wolves?"

Buck slowly shook his head. "A bear, I suspect, looking for a place to hibernate. They can be ornery critters. Go on, now. Take it nice and easy and turn Diana around."

Bears, wolves, what's next in wonderful Montana?

Chapter Twenty

"Good boy, Black," Buck said after Joz guided her horse to face downhill.

She looked over her shoulder, aware Buck was keeping his eyes peeled downwind. He saw the brush moving parallel to and behind them before she did.

"Oh, damn—a mama bear and a cub," he hissed. "Listen, Joz: I'll fire in the air to scare the mama. As soon as I do, give Diana a kick and start a lope toward home. Tell her to 'go home.' She'll understand. She'll carry you straight to the ranch."

"What about you?"

"I'll be along. Most bears run from shooting—let's hope this one does." He aimed toward the scrub bush but sighted above the trees. "Black, stand."

The horse obeyed perfectly. Buck fired, the sound like a firecracker in the quiet.

Joz kicked her horse gently. "Go, Diana! Go home."

Diana's gait was smooth, making it easy for Joz to hang on without much strength in her leg muscles. She thought for an instant about how much she loved riding and how naturally it was coming back, but as Diana rounded the bend it occurred to her that she didn't hear Black behind her. She looked over her shoulder. Sure enough, Buck wasn't back there.

Should I go back?

She started to, but she could almost hear Buck implore her to continue. Keeping a good clip down the incline, Diana didn't slow until the barn came into view. Joz rode Diana all the way to the cabin and dismounted on the porch, taking advantage of the short drop to mitigate the back and shoulder pain. Ordinarily, she would have walked the horse to the stable, but now she was frightened of what might have happened to Buck. Tying Diana to a fencepost for the moment, she shoved open the front door.

"James! Bond!" she called out. "Find Daddy! Find Buck!" To her surprise (and great relief), the dogs scampered outside with their noses in the air. "That way, boys!" she added, lifting her arm and pointing northwest. The dogs took off, and Joz ran inside and grabbed her phone and a hunting rifle, filling her pockets with ammunition. She remembered to grab a bottle of water and easily mounted Diana this time.

"I know you're tired, girl," she said to the horse, "but we need to find Buck and Black. Go, Diana!"

The horse responded well, galloping strongly up the incline. Joz slowed her to a lope at the top. Suddenly, Black came galloping toward her without Buck, passing her by with terrified eyes.

Oh, God. Buck's alone with that damned bear. "Hurry, Diana! Hurry!"

The horse galloped around the bend. Up ahead, the dogs barked and snarled at something out of sight. Joz eased Diana forward, aware of sweat dripping from her temples, and saw movement in the brush—hopefully the dogs had chased the bears away from Buck. Then she saw him. He was lying on the trail. Completely still.

****

"Whoa, Diana." Joz slid her feet from the stirrups and came out of the saddle, lowering herself to the ground. She loaded the rifle and cocked it just in case. Then she knelt by Buck's side. "Buck? Are you okay? Speak to me."

A long moment seemed to pass, though it was probably no more than several seconds before his eyes fluttered open. "Joz," he uttered. "Wow... I hit my head, I think."

She gasped when she saw his leg. The bear had shredded his jeans. There were multiple gashes above his right knee, and the pant leg was a bloody mess. She yanked off her scarf and began tying off the most serious wound.

"You're hurt. I'll try to be gentle."

"Let me." He took the scarf from her to attend to his leg wound. "You won't be able to tie it tight enough."

She watched, aghast, as he applied surprising force while tying off the gash above his knee. Given his loss of blood, she had no idea where the strength came from, nor how he could stand the pain.

"Damn mama bear. After I fired, she came up from behind—damn thing moves amazingly quietly for such a big animal. She knocked me clean off and gave Black a mean swat. She kept her at bay until the dogs took over." Buck shifted his weight so he could face her. He was pale and had broken out in a cold sweat—probably in intense pain. "If you hadn't sent James and Bond, I'd be a goner. I thought I heard my rifle hit a rock. I didn't see where it went."

"I see it, but we've more important things to worry about like getting you to a hospital."

"Find me a strong branch to use as a crutch," he said,

breathing heavily.

"No way. I'll help you mount Diana." She handed him the water bottle. "Drink."

He took several gulps before handing it back to her. "That horse is too little to carry both of us, Joz."

"Then I'll walk alongside. I'm sure the dogs chased off the bears." She helped him to his feet, but he didn't look good as he balanced on one leg. He held Joz's good shoulder to stay upright. "I'll mount with my usable leg," he said. "I'll need you to pull the hurt leg over. Don't be shy—just do it."

Joz nodded. Buck gave a hop and slipped his left leg into the stirrup. Then he gritted his teeth, seeming to call upon all the strength he had left, and leaned over the saddle by using his hand to pull his wounded leg up and halfway over. He swiveled his head around, facing the same way as Diana, and nodded at Joz. She gently pulled his leg over the stirrup.

God, help me get him home in one piece, and please protect the dogs. "Ready? I'll call nine-one-one right now."

Buck nodded, alarmingly pale. Joz took hold of the reins and walked Diana quickly down the trail. Thankfully the call went right through.

"I'm on the Double L Ranch," she said when the operator asked what her emergency was. It took all her concentration to speak slowly and explain well. "A bear attacked the owner, Buck Bigelow. I'm bringing him down the trail, but it might take fifteen minutes to get to the house. Please send an ambulance to meet us. His leg is torn up badly, and he's lost a lot of blood... hello?"

Joz looked at the phone screen, which read NO SERVICE.

Oh, no. I sure hope they heard everything.

****

Joz, trying her best to stay calm, breathed deeply while walking Diana. Every few steps she looked up at Buck, who managed to hang on to the horse but looked worse with each passing second. It took twenty minutes, but the ranch house finally came into view and—Thank God!—a rescue vehicle was coming down the drive. She hadn't seen Black and hoped the stallion had returned to its stall.

Glancing at her phone, she saw that she had cell service and called nine-one-one again. After identifying herself, she told the operator to tell the EMT to look up the hill to the northwest. It took several seconds, but the driver leaned out of the vehicle and looked in her direction. She waved, and the driver waved back and maneuvered the rescue vehicle over to them. Two young, physically fit men emerged and helped Buck dismount. He was breathing, but his eyes were closed.

"I need to put the horse in the barn," she said to the EMT closest to her. "Where are you taking Buck? I'm visiting and don't know the area well."

"Kalispell Regional."

"I'll find it. Please hurry." After a quick prayer for Buck's recovery, she tied Diana to the same fencepost she'd used earlier and looked around the yard.

There was no sign of Black.

Chapter Twenty-One

The last place Joz planned to check before conceding that Black was gone was the barn. She felt obligated to find Buck's valuable stallion and see him safely to shelter, but the horse had clearly made its feelings known about her—Joz knew she would be in serious trouble if she encountered the huge animal in a tight space. But if he'd really been spooked by that bear, he might have gone in any direction.

Circling the structure, she saw that Buck had closed the front barn door but left the rear one open, probably for ventilation. It was possible that Black may have jumped inside the paddock and retreated to the safety of his stall—horses were smart animals.

She went back to the fencepost and untied Diana, then walked her slowly to the front of the barn. Taking a deep breath, she stepped inside. The donkeys gave away her position immediately, sticking out their heads and hee-hawing for food the moment Joz and Diana were inside. That drew the attention of Black, which sent an equal mix of relief and fear through Joz.

"God, he did jump in," she said. Black reared in his stall and trotted straight for Joz, ears laid back, nostrils flaring. She grabbed Diana's stall door, shoved the horse through, and swung it shut. "Move, Diana," Joz snapped, nudging the horse again. This gave her room to slide the lock shut, stepping out of range of the stallion rearing and baring his teeth.

I'm safe with Diana. "Easy, Black. Easy, big boy."

Black pounded the floor with both hooves. Ignoring the stallion, Joz removed Diana's bridle and saddle as total exhaustion hit. She dropped the equipment in the corner, figuring a blanket would keep Diana comfortable.

Maybe food would calm Black down.

Black was still pawing the ground but didn't seem quite as fierce. Looking around, Joz saw that she could climb over the partition between the stalls to the feed sacks and slide them down. Maybe she could coax Black into his pen with some grub and somehow lock him inside.

"Diana, how about a snack?"

The horse nuzzled Joz's neck. Summoning strength she didn't think she had, she managed to fill a bucket of oats and poured some of it into Diana's trough. Aware Black was watching, Joz took care of the two donkeys next. Then, after a quick peek at Black (who was clearly interested in the food), she climbed toward his trough and managed to empty the bucket. Backing away, she watched Black snort before he hurried into his stall.

Suddenly needing air, Joz reached inside her jacket and fumbled with her inhaler before getting it into her mouth and taking a puff. Knowing she didn't have long, she slipped open the donkeys' pen and peered at Black— he was eating heartily. She scurried to his stall door in a crouch, swinging the door shut when the big horse, moving impossibly fast, whirled, and charged. She slid the lock closed just as Black thrust his mouth toward her. He missed by inches, the clack as his big teeth came together sending a spike of fear down her spine.

"Don't bite the hand that feeds you, Black," she snapped. "Now go on."

The horse turned to feed. Joz got a good look at the red stripe down his hind quarter and felt her eyes widen. The bear had raked him good.

"Oh, damn," she said, her anger at the stallion dissipating. "I know that hurts. Let me see what I can do."

Joz walked slowly back to the cabin, her exhaustion really kicking in. She drank down a glass of water, then found Buck's whiskey. "Hmm," she said aloud. "I could pour some of this on the wound, provided he doesn't kick me to kingdom come."

She thought about it another second, gauging the risk, but she couldn't let the big stallion suffer—the ugly wound would likely get infected, and then Black would really be in a bad way. Gathering apples, carrots, and sugar cubes into a leather bag she found in the supply room, she threw the bag over her shoulder. She grabbed the whiskey before noticing a big tube of ointment. She took this as well, figuring Buck had treated horses before in just this way many times before. The key would be staying calm, and she vowed to project strength as she strode back out to the barn.

"Hello, Black."

He gave her a warning snort, flattened his ears, and snapped at her. She was ready and darted backward, then reached into the bag for an apple and took a bite.

"It's for you, buddy. If you want some, here you go."

She threw the rest of her apple inside the gate and walked toward the door. After Black went for the treat and devoured it, Joz stepped back toward him and tossed several carrots deeper into the stall. She'd planned this well—the stallion had to turn to eat them, and now his hind end was pressed against the stall door. Her heart beating fast, Joz uncapped the whiskey and climbed onto the second rung. Reaching up, she tilted the bottle and let alcohol soak the wound.

"These are all yours." She tossed the remainder of the treats to the stall floor. Black ate hungrily, and Joz decided there was no time like the present and gobbed ointment onto the wound. He continued eating without any reaction she could see.

"I wish you'd let me take off that saddle," she said softly. Then she spotted the cinch—it was reachable through the slats in the gate. She opened the buckle, making the girth hang. Maybe the saddle would fall off, she thought. Black finally snorted, but this one sounded more tired than fierce.

"If I can get one of your reins and hook it downward, you can't bite me. Okay, Black?" The horse turned to the stall door with angry ears. "Still don't trust me? I saved the best for last."

Black stepped forward cautiously and put his big head over the stall door. She extended both hands: the left to feed him, the right to take his reins. Two cubes were in her hand, which gave her the extra second she needed. Black snapped up the sugar, and Joz efficiently pulled down the reins and tied them on a hook that kept his head down but over the door. Then she stood on a rung, reached above her head, and pulled the bridle over Black's ears. When he turned to the rear of his stall, the saddle slid off.

"Good boy, Black. You're free!" She filled each bay

with hay, making certain to fill the water troughs before shutting both barn doors. Limping to the porch, she dialed information, asking for the number to Kalispell Regional Hospital. Talking to a hospital employee, she described Buck Bigelow and referred to him as her husband, but as soon as she said "attacked by a bear," the employee immediately knew who the patient was.

"Is this Joz?"

"Yes, that's me—how is he?"

"Sleeping now, and he'll stay overnight for observation. He wanted to leave as soon as we stitched him up, but we weren't having that, not with that big knot on his head."

Joz felt herself relax and even break into a smile. "Tell him all the animals are safely fed and bedded down. I'll call tonight to check on him, if that's okay."

"Of course, ma'am," the man said. "I'll let him know."

She thanked him and hung up as James and Bond stepped onto the porch and looked at her expectantly. She'd forgotten all about them and hurried into the cabin to feed them and pour fresh water. Both dogs were filthy, smelled awful, and looked exhausted—Bond even held his front left paw off the floor as he ate.

Grunting as she dropped to her knees, Joz inspected the paw and saw a picker an inch long protruding from it. She got a good grip and yanked it out. Bond barked and pulled his paw away, but a second later he put full weight on it and resumed eating. Vowing to bathe the dogs after she got some rest—they probably saved both our lives—Joz collapsed into an armchair near the fireplace to remove her boots. They wouldn't come off.

"Whatever," she said wearily. She thought about a

shot of Buck's whiskey but settled on a glass of wine to help her stressed muscles relax. After the dogs had eaten and drank, they settled near the fireplace in a heap. Joz, too tired now to even go upstairs and crawl into bed, pulled the hassock close to the chair and propped up her feet. She finished the wine, set down the glass, and closed her eyes.

****

Joz watched from a beach she didn't recognize as Frank captained a speed boat. Her heart surged—he was coming toward her, and they would finally be reunited—but her view began to widen. Another speed boat was now in view as a helicopter zoomed down, Joz only now associating the flapping sound with the small craft. She watched in horror as men emerged with rifles. She wanted to run into the water, desperate to protect Frank if she could, but she couldn't move her feet. His craft exploded then, sending a fireball into the air.

Joz felt herself scream more than she heard it, but she must have screamed because James was on his hind legs licking her face when she came to.

"Thank you, James. What an awful dream," she said, wiping tears from her eyes.

She wobbled up the stairs, made it to her bed, and tried again to remove her boots once in a sitting position. They still wouldn't come off. Cursing aloud, she collapsed into the bed fully clothed and closed her eyes.

Chapter Twenty-Two

A bum leg wasn't going to keep him in the hospital, Buck decided before sunup, especially with a ranch to tend. He got himself dressed, quietly called a driver to carry him home, and arrived at the cabin just after sunrise. He was surprised to find the front door unlocked, and he couldn't believe how bad James and Bond smelled—it was almost enough to jostle the precarious balance he had on his crutches.

"It's great to see you, too, boys," he said to the dogs, whose cropped tails wagged in almost perfect unison. "Thanks for helping me out yesterday, and your reward will be a nice, hot bath. Now go pee—go on." He watched the dogs scurry out into the front yard, then checked the living room. "Joz?"

No answer. He checked his watch, knowing it was early but surprised she didn't call the hospital last night. A nurse reported that Joz had called shortly after he was examined by the doctor and said to let him know that the animals were all fine. That was good to know, but had Joz overdone it yesterday? She was recovering from her own injury (thanks to Black), not to mention the difficult time she was having with the separation from Frank.

He'd been on crutches before and managed the stairs with ease, thinking about how handy they'd come in once while doing undercover work. He carefully maneuvered the stairs and eased down the hall, looking through the open door of the guest bedroom. Joz was snoozing peacefully. It looked like she'd dropped right into bed fully clothed. He felt a wave of affection for her and approached quietly.

"Joz? You okay?"

"Hmm… what?" Her eyes opened. "Buck—you're home."

"I hired a cab."

"But how—"

"The leg is stitched up. No serious damage. I'll keep an eye out for infection and use these sticks," he said, lifting the right crutch and gesturing with it. "One bear claw almost hit the bone, but thankfully no nerve damage."

"That's good."

He tapped her right boot with his crutch. "You fall into bed exhausted, snockered, or both?"

She winced as she sat up. "Not snockered, but incredibly weary. I hurt all over."

"I'll go check on the horses, and I've already told the dogs a bath is in their near future." He tapped her boot again. "Then I'll whip us up some breakfast. Assuming you feel like getting up, that is."

"Buck?"

"Yes?"

"Breakfast would be great—first, could you pull off these boots? I couldn't budge them. I don't know why…"

He smiled, then balanced on his crutches while leaning over enough to reach the boots. He removed them with quick flicks of his wrists and dropped them on the floor. "There you go, young lady," he said. "Over breakfast you can tell me how you handled Black."

****

Joz stayed in bed another minute, thinking. She remembered the dream about Frank—the poor dog was consoling her when she came to—and she recalled making it up the stairs and into bed. Attempting to stand sent a stab of pain through her and brought her to the present. What she would give for Frank to be here and take care of her, she thought, as she limped into the bathroom. She took a long look at her horrid self in the mirror above the sink and visualized Frank embracing her from behind.

You will sure get a piece of my mind when we're together again, mister, and you ask how much I liked the great state of Montana.

****

Black and Diana whinnied and the donkeys made their usual racket when Buck stepped into the barn. "Good morning, all," he said, touching Black before the others. The horse expected to be acknowledged first and searched Buck's coat for a sugar cube. Buck pulled out two of them.

"You earned these, Black. You hung in for me and gave that bear hell before the dogs took over. Let's look… no, that hind end wound isn't deep. Did you let that gal get under your skin, boy? You ought to—she's nice and brave, even took care of you, too. We'll give the wound another cleaning today."

Buck managed to pluck Black's saddle from the stall floor while balancing on his crutches, though putting pressure on his wounded leg sent a jolt of pain through him that brought tears to his eyes. Then he returned the saddle to the tack room as Black patiently waited for his master's okay to go outside. His horse tore into the corral, kicking out his hind end. Buck opened Diana's stall handing over a pair of sugar cubes to the much mellower horse.

"Joz thinks the donkeys are cute, Diana," he said. "Actually, I think Joz is cute. What do you think of that, girl?" He gently slapped Diana's flank. "Now go out there and play with your buddy." Diana trotted out into the sunlight. Buck gave each donkey a treat next, then sent them outside before walking carefully back to the cabin, not wanting to jar his leg again. Joz stepped out onto the porch as he approached.

"You okay? Anything you need?"

"No, I'm done. Let's eat!"

"I took the liberty of making coffee," she said. "It's strong."

"My kitchen, Joz," he said, following her inside.

"Yes, that's a violation, but under the circumstances—"

"Certainly forgivable this time. I'm hungry as a bear."

Joz was in the middle of a sip and laughed, sending coffee down her chin and sweatshirt. "Very funny, Buck."

"That just popped out—the mama sure had a temper. If you hadn't let the dogs out, you'd be cooking breakfast for yourself from now on."

Her smile disappeared. "Not funny, Buck."

"Well, I did choose a new favorite song. May I?" He broke into a warbly baritone, "Who let my Aussies out? You, you, you!"

At least that made her smile. *I sure stepped in it with the cooking-for-one comment.* He watched as she seemed to turn serious again.

"It all happened so fast," she said. "I can't remember anything but having to focus on you—and I was so frightened."

"Hey, I'm supposed to be taking care of you, and instead you saved my life. So thank you, Joz. You risked everything coming for me. I appreciate it more than you know."

"How could I not?" she asked, genuinely surprised.

"Oh, some gals would'a froze in that situation. Some might have been too afraid to return. But Frank said you were special."

He almost didn't add the comment, because—as he knew it would—it brought a warm smile and high color to her cheeks. He'd given Frank his word that he would never attempt anything inappropriate with Joz or allow himself to develop feelings for her, but it was hard to deny the stirrings he felt this morning. After all, he thought, they'd survived real terror up there in the woods. They could easily have been killed.

"Well, I'm glad he thinks so," she said. "Now, I'd offer to set the table—or help cook breakfast—but I know how you feel about your kitchen."

"I've got it under control." He balanced on his crutches and started for the kitchen. "Stay put and relax."

****

As Buck fussed in the kitchen, Joz thought about her dream and wondered if she should share it with him. It struck her as something she would certainly discuss—the men were close friends—but something she couldn't put her finger on told her not to. At least for now.

She was content to savor the wonderful smells coming from the kitchen while alone with her thoughts.

Buck walked in later with a heaping plate of food. She gasped when she realized what it was.

"I believe Eggs Benedict is your favorite," he said, presenting the dish with as much of a flourish as he could manage on his crutches.

Frank obviously shared my tastes with him. She forked in a bite and closed her eyes. "Oh, Buck, this is mind-blowing. Wow, this is good."

"Thank you. As I told you, my kitchen—I can cook up good chow."

She had to admit she liked his smile, which she noticed between bites, and she was secretly flattered when he pointed out that her pinky finger stood at attention each time she sipped coffee. He was clearly paying attention to her.

"You're a good cook. Just please don't make this often, Buck. I gain weight faster than a corn-fed hog."

"Nothing's wrong with a few extra pounds, young lady."

"I wish that were true. Trust me—I've put on weight before, and everything begins to hurt. And why, if you don't mind, do you call me 'young lady'? You've done that more than once."

Buck smiled again. "The obvious: you're younger than me. Also, you look young, and seem youthful. You strike me as serious when you need to be, but fun whenever you can be. You seem carefree, other than being away from Frank. And you have a great smile."

A great smile? The last comment surprised her, almost to the point of discomfort. She looked away for an instant. "I mean, good grief, Buck… you're cooking for me, doing my laundry… got those silly boots off me. I suppose Frank gave you the keys and paperwork to my

St. Croix building?"

"No. He said the management company takes care of everything, and you'd get a monthly deposit in your account. I assume you've been checking on it?"

"Yes. It's there." She took a long look at him. "Do you miss being an agent?"

"Not at all. I enjoyed being married—ball and chain and all." He smiled to let her know he was kidding, and this smile looked more natural. "Some men need the thrill of pulling off the impossible, bullets flying. I did in my youth, but I was eager to retire."

"You sure you don't miss the excitement?"

"Joz, I had enough yeehaw yesterday. And I've got to rest this dern leg. If you're looking for something to do, we can read, watch a movie, or hang out. Around noon I'll put fresh antibiotics on Black's rump. Thanks again for doing such a great job with him."

"Least I could do. And reading sounds like a great idea."

"Join me if you want. I like the den because the critters are in view.

"That sounds like a plan—and Buck?"

He was starting to clear the table and paused to look up.

"I'm relieved you're okay."

"Thank you, Joz—"

Is that color in his cheeks?

"—and I'm greatly relieved you're okay too."

Chapter Twenty-Three

Spring in Montana didn't look much different than winter as far as Joz was concerned. While there were hints of green on the trees and some pretty pinks and yellow on the rose bushes by late March, Buck had informed her that it was often June before what she would think of as warmer weather would be here. The snow-capped mountains in the distance looked just as foreboding as they had at Thanksgiving, Christmas, and New Year's when they toasted to Frank's wellbeing.

She continued to nurture the hope that Frank would contact her soon, announcing that his mysterious assignment had ended. But the nightmare she'd had months earlier about Frank being killed in the boat attack returned periodically, and one morning she woke up bathed in sweat. Something was wrong—she could almost feel it in her bones. And Buck was on it when she came down the stairs in the plush robe Frank sent when she first got here.

"I'm guessing it's a three-coffee morning," he said from the kitchen.

"It's the robe, I'm sure," she said, joining him.

He presented her with a steaming mug. "Have a seat. Your timing is perfect—breakfast is ready." She took in the heavenly smells. At least she had an appetite, and her mouth watered at the poached eggs, muffin half, and

Canadian bacon with a diet hollandaise on the side.

"Gosh, thank you, Frank. You're a wonder." Joz realized what she'd done and kicked herself internally. "What a horrible night," she said. "I never knew how hazardous dreaming could be."

Buck's countenance dimmed. "Tell me about it."

"Why? You know who it's about."

"Purge it from your system before you call me Frank again."

"Buck—"

"Tell me in detail, Joz. In living color."

She forked in a bite of eggs and savored the taste. "It's the same basic nightmare I've had before—"

"Which you've never told me about."

"—okay. There's water, a chase, an explosion, a fire, and a boat sinking. That Frank's on, of course. He's calling for me, but I'm watching from the shore and I can't move to help him. It's awful."

"You said you had this dream before. How long have you had it?"

"The first time was right around when the bear attacked."

Buck munched on a strip of bacon. "I wish you'd told me before now."

"I always overcook or undercook poached eggs. But you make them perfectly. Soft on the inside with the tiniest bit of runny yolk."

"Don't change the subject. I'm guessing you're empathic to some degree, maybe an unpracticed psychic? I'm serious, Joz."

"My mother had prophetic dreams that were sometimes spot on, but they don't come easily for me and need interpretation." She washed down her bite of egg with a sip of coffee and faced him. "Okay. I'm going to ask you a very direct question, and I want an honest answer."

Whatever Buck was feeling, she noticed, he didn't change expression. "Ask away."

"Is Frank really in trouble, or am I just missing him like crazy?"

"Your husband is always in trouble."

"His work is serious business," she said with an edge in her voice. "You know that as well as anyone, and now is not the time for humor."

"You don't understand, little lady. In the past, Frank took things to the edge, and we all thought he was a goner. He said, 'That's what a con requires for success.' He thrived on pushing the envelope like a thrill-seeking pilot. That's the Frank I know."

Joz let her shoulders slump. He wasn't answering her question—not directly, anyway. "But he's not a young man. He wouldn't possibly risk everything, including our relationship, for some sort of thrill… would he?"

Buck had never felt more at a crossroads in his life. His coffee burbled in his stomach as he considered what to say and how to say it. It would be easier to break this sweet lady's heart—a hell of a lot easier—if he hadn't fallen for Joz. He had, and in a big way, despite Frank's warning not to develop feelings for her. Gazing into her eyes, he made a decision he hoped he wouldn't regret.

God help me. Still trying to frame his thoughts, he held off speaking when Joz leaned forward impatiently. "Frank didn't tell you about what an agent goes through before a uniquely dangerous mission, did he?"

"Of course not, except that a partner screwed up a

job years ago and some Chinese syndicate threatened England. He had to fix it."

Buck held her eyes. "Even that small piece of knowledge, you shouldn't know. Frank trusts you completely to have shared that, but he failed to tell you something else about preparing for a critical mission—and, unfortunately, left that part to me."

He had her complete attention and felt himself weaken. Her senses were on high alert, the smile on her face as brittle as fine china. He stalled by clearing the table and refilling their coffee mugs, trying to nail down his true motivation.

To get her angry at Frank so I might have a future with her? It's about time she knows, anyway.

"So tell me already, Buck!"

"Let's mosey into the den. The critters love the new snowfall."

"Sure, as long as you don't change the subject this time."

Joz took the end of the couch closest to the fireplace. Buck sat four feet away and watched Black prance in the snow. Diana rolled on her back as if breakdancing. She did that often, and it usually drew a big smile from Joz—but not this time. She was dead serious as she turned to him, both hands on her cup.

"I don't like your demeanor at all. Am I going to need your hundred-proof this early in the day?"

"Possibly. You understand that the agency is an elite group, beyond secret," Buck said. "You shouldn't be aware of their existence or methods, but I will tell you one important thing that Frank kept from you." She said nothing and backed as far into her end of the couch as she could.

"Every so often, an operation's high level of danger puts family members in harm's way. In case the enemy captures their operative, the agency eliminates the threat to itself and family members by erasing all personal information from the operative's brain." Buck paused, letting the words sink in. "That way, the agent—not even under the threat of torture—won't reveal anything personal that the enemy might use against the agency, including family members."

"I don't understand," she said tonelessly.

"Through drugs and suggestions—a kind of brainwashing if you will—a professional will purge relationships from the agent's memory."

Joz's eyes grew in horror. She understood now. He was surprised she held onto her coffee cup.

"Family, girlfriends, and wives... they don't exist for Frank anymore," Buck added. "He is an agent with a job to do. He retains memories of the agency, me, and his work—but that is all he knows."

"No, no, no! Frank wouldn't give me up—give us up—not for a freaking job! Not for a damned adventure!"

Buck set his cup on the coffee table, then scooted close and took Joz's free hand. "Of course he wouldn't. But Frank would do anything to keep you and his country safe. He's English through and through, and had he refused to help, both of you could be dead by now." He paused, wanting to make his next words come out exactly the right way. "He didn't leave you for an adventure, Joz. Frank left to protect you and his country. Always remember that."

Tears streamed down her cheeks. "But after he succeeds... after he comes home... memories will surface… right?"

Buck knew that it would be worse than cruel to continue. The hard truth was that Frank's first two wives were erased during high-stakes operations. Joz didn't need to know that, nor did she need to learn that Buck had helped Frank with a previous wife who flew home to Los Angeles after seeing firsthand that her husband had absolutely no idea who she was.

"They complete a clearing, Joz, when the job is high-risk," he said. "The communists must win at all costs—they will use or eliminate anyone, including family, to achieve their goals. The agency, in undertaking such a clearing, makes that impossible for them."

"Answer me, Buck," she growled, aiming an index finger at him. "Will his memories of me—and our love—return to him?"

He forced himself to look at the broken woman. "No. I'm sorry."

Joz jumped to her feet. Buck could see her shaking and knew she was about to erupt. "So this is all a sham," she said, her voice low and tight. "Me waiting here in Montana with you, waiting endlessly—waiting foolishly—for the love of my life to return. Isn't it?"

"It's keeping you alive, Joz. That's God's honest truth."

I hate you, Buck, with every fiber of my being.

The words were on the tip of her tongue. She settled for absolutely slicing him to ribbons with her eyes.

"I'd rather face the enemy," she said, spitting the word, "than face betrayal by the one man I trusted one hundred percent, the man who held my heart in his hands. And you—you knew all this time Frank wouldn't recognize me after he came home?!? I came to trust you like I trusted Frank! That's a huge step for me—a damned colossal step—and now, while serving me a gourmet breakfast, you reveal how easily lies come to you as well!"

"I promised Frank—"

"What about me? We're friends, Buck. We're confidants... aren't we?"

Buck started to speak, then turned away. Before she thought better of it, she grabbed her cup and threw it at his head. What was left of her coffee flew in droplets as the mug sailed over her target and shattered on the shale floor behind him.

"How could you?" she sputtered. "How could my Frank?"

She stormed toward the front door, needing fresh air. Buck, on his feet quickly, grabbed her. She tried to push away, but he was too strong—he held her firmly in place until she slumped against his chest and sobbed. Then he walked her back to the couch.

"Please sit," he said quietly. "We aren't through talking."

"There's nothing to talk about. I'll never forgive you."

"Please sit," he repeated. He grabbed the whiskey, uncapped it, and took a small sip before handing it to her. "Just a sip—right out of the bottle."

She took two before he gently took the bottle from her and put the cap back on. She said she needed her inhaler, and he got up and trotted upstairs for it. The medication helped clear her lungs, and she held onto a throw pillow like it was a life preserver.

"What am I going to do?" She couldn't face Buck.

"Where will I live? I can't go to St. Croix and relive precious memories without Frank."

"I know this is the very last thing you want to hear, but I'm not sure I've ever done anything as hard as telling you what I just did," he said after a long pause. "Frank wanted me to wait a full year—"

Joz's mouth fell open. This felt like another knife slashing through her, though Buck's liquor had dulled some of the pain.

"—no way I could do that, Joz. Part of me wanted to tell you the day after you got here, once you'd gotten some rest and a good meal. But you were clearly suffering, and I couldn't add to it. I put it off and put it off, trying somehow to find the right way to break the news. I couldn't watch you agonize anymore after seeing you this morning."

"I'll pack my things, go live with my son for a while. He believes Frank and I are still traveling," she said with a snort.

"I can't allow that, Joz. You are to stay at my home to keep everyone safe, including your son. Try to remember that, please."

Unbelievable. "Okay... so when his mission is through, will Frank show up just to ignore me? Is that how this little game works?"

"Frank left instructions for the agency to contact me. He wanted me to tell you about his memory loss if he made it through... but not if he didn't—"

Anger spiked through her veins and she whirled. "Did he, now?"

"—we may not hear of the results for some time. And Joz, I couldn't go that route because I've come to care about you," he said huskily. "I'm saying I couldn't

140

treat a friend that way, certainly not a friend who saved my life."

She turned away. Buck sure didn't feel like a friend at the moment, but there was nothing to gain from being unnecessarily ugly.

"You don't have to decide anything now," he said. "My house is your home, for whatever amount of time you wish to stay."

"I'd like to be alone right now."

"Then you stay here, and I'll go check on the animals." He stood and started for the door. When James and Bond (who'd apparently scurried into the kitchen after she threw the coffee cup) realized their master was about to go outside, they scampered after him. Joz waited until Buck had closed the door before easing her head onto the pillow. She lay on her side, staring at what she hoped was the last snowfall of the season. She felt as cold and empty inside as it looked beyond the window.

Chapter Twenty-Four

The next few days passed without a spoken word between them. Buck continued to cook delicious breakfasts for Joz and left them in the oven on low heat, along with plenty of coffee, before heading out to do his chores around the ranch. He seemed to understand that she needed space and spent entire days snowplowing, repairing fence posts, and fixing hinges.

One morning she watched from the living room window as James and Bond jumped into snow drifts in search of mice hidden underneath, and the sight of the dogs standing on their hind legs while Buck rubbed his hands together thawed her heart a bit.

"He must be freezing," she said to herself. "He's treated me with so much kindness, so much respect. This isn't his fault—it's Frank's." Before talking herself out of it, she tugged on her boots, slipped on her coat, poured a hot mug of coffee, and strolled out to the barn.

"Well, hello there," Buck said with a smile when he saw her.

"I brought you some coffee. Once I saw the critters with their blankets on, I figured you could use a warm-up."

"That's very kind, Joz. Are you warm enough?"

"Yes. I hardly feel the chill."

"That's the danger of western winters. Early settlers

froze to death because they didn't understand how important it is to dress for warmth despite not feeling the freezing temperatures."

"I like the dryness," she said, more comfortable around him than she would have anticipated. "I froze when I lived by the ocean in winter, so I moved to Florida and the islands. But winter here is surprisingly bearable—I wish it didn't last so doggone long."

He smiled but didn't reply. She knew he didn't want to say the wrong thing. And it was up to her to continue the conversation, whether that meant small talk or following through on what she decided on. "I apologize for acting like a child, Buck. I've never thrown a dish in my life."

"It was a mug—and I deserved it."

"No, you didn't. Frank caused this. I'm grateful for your kindness and hospitality. I appreciate and understand how close you and Frank are."

"We're like brothers." He looked off into the barn before facing her again. "But that doesn't excuse me from withholding information. Maybe I should have told you earlier, but I thought you'd take off for the islands and get yourself killed. And I'd never forgive myself if that happened."

"I understand, and I've learned one thing for certain—" She gave him a rueful smile. "—never fall in love with a member of a clandestine service unless he is fully retired."

He didn't reply and looked away. She left him sitting on a hay bale, not needing to know what he was thinking. She'd said her piece, she thought, and started for the barn door.

"Are we okay, Joz?" he called out.

"Absolutely."

The door stuck. So much for a graceful exit. She gave it a swift kick, which got it open... and caused a snowdrift on the roof to loosen and descend on her as she stepped outside. She was up to her waist in the snow before she could react.

Buck burst into laughter and took his time going over to her. Embarrassed, she was about to respond when James and Bond sprinted past him, launched, and threw themselves at her. This knocked Joz over and caused Buck to laugh even harder.

"You look like a powder-covered pastry!"

"How about helping me up?"

He held out a hand and got her to her feet. The second she was out of the snowdrift, she plastered his face with a snowball she'd hastily made.

"Now we're even," she said with a smile. She slipped her arm into his. "Come on, let's go inside before we freeze out here."

They strolled to the house—like an old married couple—but it felt right. So did her apology and Buck's reaction to it; he was graceful enough to say little as she tested out her comfort level at being around him again.

The pleasing moment ended quickly when the dogs turned to the hill and growled. Joz turned and glanced in the direction of the route they'd taken the day the bear attacked. Buck, she saw, was staring discreetly. Then he nodded for her to go inside and shoved James and Bond into the cabin when they hesitated. Without a word to her, he strode to his oak gun rack.

"What's going on?" she asked.

He pulled a lever and spun the rack around. Frank's collection was impressive, but the opposite side of

Buck's gun rack included automatic weapons she'd never seen before.

"These are modified automatics I made myself," he said. "A hobby of mine that came in handy as an agent."

"Doesn't look like you're fully retired."

Buck didn't smile and motioned her close. "Listen to me: someone is spying on us from the hills—I saw the sun glint off something up there. I don't know what went wrong; maybe someone didn't buy Frank's story about your divorce and our marriage. I'm thinking his mission didn't go as expected."

Her heart dropped. "No, Buck—"

His cell phone buzzed, silencing them. He grabbed it, looked at the call screen, and answered. Joz could hear a deep voice talking very fast.

"Of course I remember you, George, and let me cut in—you've called too late if you're issuing a warning. Someone's already watching here. He'll probably wait until nightfall to attack."

Joz backed away, trying to take in the information without having a full-blown panic attack.

"George, it isn't me we're concerned about. It's time you break protocol and call for backup—think of it as a distraction if you wish—if for no other reason than to protect Frank's innocent wife. As you know, she has been here for more than six months."

Joz couldn't make out anything the man named George said in response, but she didn't like Buck's frown. His expression turned to one of resignation before he said, which he did politely given the circumstances. He ended the call and went back to checking his weapons. She stepped close to him and demanded to know what was going on.

"We are under attack," he said ominously.

"Go on."

"Frank is missing—his ruse failed. The Chinese must have questioned his divorce story. I warned him that too many people saw the two of you together, but he couldn't come up with another plan as fast as needed, apparently." Buck looked up from his guns. "Keep James and Bond in the house at all times, Joz. If they're outside they'll go right to the stranger to check him out, and we can't have that."

"Will do."

"I'll equip us with some of the rifles. If you use one, just pull the trigger—there's no safety or lock."

"Got it. What do these people want from us?"

He sighed. "Not from me—from you."

"What are you talking about?"

Buck went hurriedly about the room, clearly looking for planted listening devices. This sent a jolt of fear down her spine. Then he walked back up to Joz, pulled her close, and placed a gentle finger on her lips. "Did Frank tell you something that you forgot to tell me?" he whispered.

"What—no!"

"Did he give you anything for safekeeping, like jewelry or a gift of any kind?"

"Yes," she said directly into his ear. "A book of sonnets by… who was it … Byron. He said to keep it with me at all times. I have it upstairs."

"Let's go have a look."

Joz watched him peer out the downstairs windows with a rifle slung over his shoulder, one in his hand, and another weapon tucked into his waistband. He barred both doors into the house, then nodded at the stairs. She went first, Buck a couple of steps behind. He followed her into the bedroom as she reached under her pillow and withdrew the book.

"He wanted me to be careful with this… and he kept saying to trust you."

"Well, Frank's plans are shot to hell. He gave you something that they want, and if it saves your life, I'll give it to them—the British and Queen be damned."

Buck took the book from her and flipped through the pages, apparently looking for underlined passages. Finding nothing, he felt the cover, then the binding.

"There it is."

He reached into his pocket and withdrew a sophisticated jackknife. Joz gasped, horrified at what he was about to do, but he placed her finger on the binder and ran it up and down—this was to let Joz know he was about to slice it open. He began at the top like Frank had, and the glue gave way as Buck's knife slid underneath it.

"It was opened before, Joz." There were tweezers within the knife's casing that allowed him to grab the small key and the piece of paper wrapped around it. Buck released a pent-up breath as he showed her the key.

"What's that for?"

"Safe deposit box and the account number with it," he said after reading the numbers on the paper. "It's a dated Swiss bank key. I suspect Frank planned for your future using the communist funds in case the operation failed."

"He would leave me stolen money?!?"

Buck said nothing. He was concentrating on the key, and she wasn't sure he'd heard her.

"Buck…?"

"Take a deep breath, Joz."

"Why?"

"Just do it, little lady."

Now really frightened, she took in a slow, deep breath, holding the air in her lungs before releasing it just as slowly. Buck faced her, a look of grim resignation on his face.

"Your dream was prophetic. George said Frank's boat did blow up. Witnesses saw money flying everywhere before the fire burned everything else on board—as the boat sank. Everyone presumes Frank died in the explosion, with the cash burning up."

"No," Joz murmured, her legs on the verge of giving way. "No, Frank…"

Buck pulled her tightly into his arms. His physical strength reminded her very much of Frank. "Don't worry—no one's found a body," he said into her ear. "Now the enemy is verifying he's dead as Frank had quite a reputation in his day for cleverness. The agency often thought him dead."

"But how—"

"Fishermen said a helicopter circled the wreckage for hours. The enemy sent divers after the fire went out, but the boat sank fast and deep in a strong current. They recovered nothing, not even a body. That sounds like a Frank maneuver. But for right now, you can bet the enemy is tying up loose ends and questioning everything, including Frank's divorce. They certainly want to question both of us."

"But we don't know anything, Buck."

"Oh, but we do. We also have something to barter with to save your life."

It took a second, but Joz realized what he meant. She backed up a step and covered her mouth. "No! Don't.

This was important to Frank—his death will be for nothing if you hand over the key—not that I believe he's dead…"

"If he is, he'll haunt me for the rest of my days if I don't save you any way possible."

Joz moved to the bed and sat down, trying to think as she imagined them being watched. "It's Friday," she said softly. "We usually go to the spring and swim. Should we keep our regular schedule? It might convey that we have no idea about them."

"True, although they could block us on the road. Or they could wait for us to leave and search the house for the key." Buck joined her on the bed. "Joz, these bastards would hunt for the proverbial needle in the haystack and, without knowing where the needle is, destroy the house and kill the critters without a second thought."

The thought of the animals being slaughtered made Joz queasy. "Then give it to them."

"I get it—no problem if we're killed, but we can't compromise the animals." He mussed her hair. "We're keeping the key, short of the threat of death for any of us on the ranch, critters included." He stood and pulled her to her feet. "I have a lightweight automatic for you to use—it was modified for Dabney—and her bulletproof vest should fit you. Put on jeans and a sweater, then come right down. We'll get you suited up. Hurry!"

****

Joz stood still as he fitted her with the vest, which he slipped over her t-shirt. She told him it felt heavy, but he said she would get used to it. She put her sweater on over the vest. Then Buck placed Dabney's gun in her hand.

"I know you're scared," he said quietly, looking into

her eyes. "But you're strong—you can handle this, Joz. Now, listen good: if a bullet hits the vest, you'll be thrown to the ground. Don't fight it—play dead. And use this twenty-two to blast those shitheads once they come close enough to hit. You with me?"

"I think so…"

"You'll have to shoot them multiple times with this peashooter, understand? Practice pulling the gun from your waistband, but if you feel capable of using the automatic, go ahead. Remember to play dead until then."

She nodded. "Frank taught me that—called it a just-in-case scenario."

Buck slapped her shoulder in approval, then strapped on his own vest and pulled his sweater over it. He placed a small pistol in his left boot and hung an assault weapon inside his winter coat. He pocketed the knives and stashed one in his right boot before handing the remaining one to her.

"Take it, Joz."

"I've never used a knife before—not like this…"

"Keep it handy. If you're placed in a rear car seat, wait until the right time to defend yourself: around a curve, or a road with trees on both sides. Stab the driver here—" He pointed to her carotid artery. "—as deep as possible."

"Okay…"

"The second fellow should grab the steering wheel to save his life. This knife goes in the sleeve of your coat, Joz—it's sharp, so be careful. Stab the enemy in the neck base and then drop to the floor, wedging yourself between the front and rear seats."

"The car's obviously going to crash—"

"Yes. Wait until it's stopped, then check yourself for

injuries before you move. If the car's still functional, use it."

"And go to?"

"The sheriff's office, or any public place with law enforcement."

"I'm glad I watched Mission Impossible and the James Bond movies," Joz said, resorting to Buck's use of injecting humor (or trying to) in stressful situations. James and Bond, hearing their names, came running into the bedroom. That made Joz laugh, and even Buck smiled.

"Hey, that's a good idea, Joz. In fact, it's brilliant."

"Yippee for me… but what did I say?"

Buck opened the back door and glared at the Australian shepherds. "Pasture, boys. Pasture!" Off they went, plowing their way through snow drifts as they ran to the corral door. Joz watched as James butted his nose up against the door's lever before Bond nosed the door open. Standing on his hind legs, Bond pushed it open wide enough for James to run inside.

"This is mind-blowing."

"Keep watching," Buck said.

The dogs got the stalls open, herding the animals outside. They used the same routine on the corral gate that opened to hundreds of acres of fields and woods.

"James and Bond are familiar with the back area," Buck said. "Feeding and watering troughs start in the lower forty. The animals and critters will smell the food that waits for them deep in the pines, and the enemy will waste time trying to locate them—they should be safe. The dogs, meanwhile, will stay until they hear my whistle."

"Okay, but what if we can't whistle?"

"The dogs will herd the critters to the barn after they run out of food. Don't worry, Joz—there's food for several weeks and an underground spring that feeds the trough. I provided adequate shelter from the weather, and remember that they wear their blankets."

"That's impressive. It really is."

"Whatever happens, save yourself. Promise me, Joz."

"I can't make a promise like that."

"We aren't talking about an ornery mama bear—please promise me. I can't concentrate on my work while worrying about you doing something stupid."

"Stupid, huh?" she teased. "Okay, I promise." *Like I'll keep it.*

"Okay, then. Use Dabney's rifle if a firefight begins while driving. Extra ammo is in the Hummer."

"So we are going to the hot spring?"

"I like your idea of sticking to our schedule. We'll leave the house wide open and show them we have nothing to hide. If they come inside and don't destroy the place, they will bug it completely—if they haven't done so already." Buck sighed. "Or they may try to run us off the road on the way to or from the spring. Now let's get our gear together and go."

****

Joz went back upstairs for her gym bag and packed it with her swimsuit and towel. Grimacing at the rifle, she hefted it, then slipped it inside the gym bag, thinking she would hide it until they were in the car. Buck was waiting for her as she came back down.

"Do we whisper in the car, too?" she asked. "Wait—where's the—"

Buck put a gentle finger on her lips to quiet her. He

leaned in. "They'll find a key, but not yours." He inserted a similar Swiss key into the binder of the Byron volume. "I used a key years ago for a booby-trapped safety deposit box, but the job was canceled."

"Oh, wow!"

"I can't promise it will work, but this should buy enough time for me to hide you." Buck pulled out his cell and made a call to an experienced ranch hand who would care for the Double L with Buck away for what he said was an undetermined period. He ended the call and looked at Joz, having said nothing to the hand about the imminent safety threat. "Let's hope I'm not putting Julio in danger. Now let's go."

Chapter Twenty-Five

Buck watched Joz while pulling his Hummer up to the front door of the cabin. He knew she was tense, but her shoulders were slumped as she came outside with her gym bag over her shoulder—he sensed sadness. Focus, pretty lady, and get your mind off Frank. At least she remembered to leave the front door unlocked, he thought, as she climbed inside.

"I need that swim," she said. "I've been lying around all week feeling sorry for myself. Frank would have kicked me in the butt to get me moving."

"He'd kick you?"

"Not literally, Buck—a gentle, verbal inspiration."

Her voice wobbled a bit, and she turned away. He started to put a reassuring hand on her shoulder but held off, afraid he'd try to embrace her. Here he was thinking Joz needed to focus, but they were as good as dead if he wasn't concentrating because of the way he felt about her.

Escaping for the moment to the hot springs still felt right. He'd packed passports and identification for them to leave the country if the situation called for it, though such a decision would be made on the fly. He'd decided not to tell Joz they might not see the cabin again—he knew she'd come to like the place and would beg forgiveness later.

Easing the Hummer down the lane, he studied the radio before turning it on softly. He turned to Joz and pointed at it.

"Didn't you say you lived on an island before moving to St. Croix?" he asked loudly. When she grimaced, he motioned exaggeratedly for her to respond.

"Amelia Island in Florida," she said. She didn't understand, and Buck's patience ebbed. He pointed firmly at the radio, then motioned again with his hand. This time her eyes widened—now she understood he'd found a bug.

"It's in the northeast part of the state," she added, projecting more. "Thought I told you that."

"You said you once lived there, babe, but I know nothing about it other than the name. How long were you there? I ask because it was mentioned on the news this morning, something about fishing."

"Thirty years, and oh, how it's changed."

He smiled and nodded for her to continue.

"When I moved to Amelia, some of the main roads were sand and woods made up half the island. It was my kind of paradise: restaurants that served southern fried *everything* and quaint bars with awesome local music. It was more like Georgia's deep south than anywhere I'd associate with Florida. But the people were great— polite, accepting, respectful."

Buck, watching the road carefully, nodded again.

"The island was virtually unknown except for the resort on the south end that held the Bausch and Lomb tennis tournaments," she said. "A girl named Christiana Efren was the tennis pro. That put Amelia on the map, unfortunately. It changed quickly from a sleepy shrimping town."

"Yeah?"

"Yeah, and yuck," Joz said. "Modern-looking homes sprouted and a bunch of northerners snapped them up, but it *really* began losing its charm when northern politicians got involved—everyone seemed to lose sight of the southern appeal that attracted so many visitors in the first place. I eventually gave up trying to fight the traffic and decided it was time to leave. I have some fantastic memories, and a few bad ones near the end."

"But you had a blast way back when."

"Oh, yeah," Joz laughed. It sounded like sincere amusement as she reflected on her life, rather than the character she was playing while they were entertaining (and hopefully throwing off) whomever was after them.

"In those days, the beach called to everyone. We socialized there, sunbathed, fished, drank, and smoked pot. All of us did. There was a lot of nightlife for such a small island. Most of it was on Centre Street, which ran from the beach to downtown. There was a huge national park with a fort open to the public—it had the *coolest* Civil War reenactments. The boating was great, too, and you can't beat riding a horse on a beach."

It was obvious that Joz was describing her own experiences, and Buck couldn't help himself. "Maybe you'll show me Amelia one day."

"And leave your critters behind?"

"I need vacations, you know. I hire dependable ranch hands and take off on a vacation every year, usually in winter."

"But you didn't go this winter because of me," she said sweetly.

"Our anniversary is important, dear. But we'll take

a vacation-slash-honeymoon next year, okay?" He winked at her, hoping she would continue to play along. "And how 'bout we drive in peaceful quiet. We can do without the music."

"I'd love that."

He switched off the radio. "Little lady, pleasing you is easy."

"As I've told you a thousand times, Buck, I'm easy to please."

****

A member of the communist party listened on headphones while interpreting the conversation Buck and Joz were having to his boss. The men were in another vehicle several miles behind.

"Prepare," the boss snapped in his native language. "Pull up Amelia Island, Florida, in case they run. Was anything found in the house?"

"Yes," the man wearing headphones said. "A key with an identification number hidden in the binding of the woman's book... a key to a Swiss deposit box."

The boss nodded firmly. "That must be it. Tell that team to meet me at the airport, and you continue to follow those two."

Chapter Twenty-Six

Buck looked up as Joz emerged from the locker room, eager to get into the hot springs and swim. He sat on a bench with a view of the entrance, discreetly watching everything and everyone, trying to look the part of a tourist as he spoke on his cell phone. But he was speaking in hushed tones to the local sheriff, a man he trusted named Roscoe.

"Joz and I decided on an impromptu trip," he said. "Julio and his family are flying in from New Mexico this evening. He'll maintain the ranch in my absence."

"Thanks for letting me know, Buck."

"I'm calling because I left the keys inside the house—would you mind sending one of your boys out to check if the door is locked or not?"

"That ain't like you. Your whiskers and your brain both turning white?"

"Sure seems that way, Roscoe. But if it's unlocked, tell your man to leave it that way, okay? And ask him to check Joz's room—the guest room upstairs with the female stuff in it. In particular, check if she left her book under the pillow. She's been fretting about it all day—doesn't go anywhere without it. I'll send him a present for the favor."

The sheriff barked a laugh. "Screw him, Buck. You donate a liter or two of that imported whiskey to me and we're good. And did I hear you say your bride sleeps in the guest room?"

"Yes," Buck groaned. "My damn snoring—she can't sleep. But she says separate rooms keeps the romance alive, and believe me, Sheriff, that's not dying anytime soon."

"I heard that."

"As to the libation, a bottle sits on the countertop by the wet bar. Help yourself, my man."

"I'll drive on over to the Double-L right now. And if the door *is* locked?"

"There's a key inside the barn door, hanging on the wall behind the horseshoe." Buck paused as an older couple walked by. "Unlock it and leave it that way, please. Call me about the door lock, if you will—and before your own brain's deteriorated from the whiskey."

****

An hour later the sheriff called back. Joz was still in the spring and working so hard that some folks lazing in the warm water were staring. Buck hadn't seen anyone who looked suspicious, nor had he overheard any snippets of conversation that caught his attention.

"Okay, Buck," Roscoe said. "You locked the front door, so I used the barn key. That book you talked about was lying on Joz's bed—*not* under her pillow—and someone apparently took a knife to the binding."

"Oh, really? I'll let Joz know. Enjoy the whiskey, Sheriff."

"I sure will, Buck. You let me know if you need anything else."

Buck thanked him, then smiled to himself after ending the call.

****

Joz's heart felt lighter after her swim, and though she was exhausted, it was the good kind of tired she'd come to anticipate after hard work on the ranch. She was back in warm clothes and bundled up and carried her gym bag to the car where Buck waited. He stepped out to open her door.

"That felt great! Gosh, I needed that. Now I need hot chocolate."

"I need some barbecue," he said. "And yes, they have hot chocolate too. It's lunchtime—let's head that way."

"Wait. I saw you on the phone a couple of times. Any news?"

He leaned close to her. "They found the key I planted, Joz."

Her eyes widened. She squeezed him tight—this development made her feel much safer. He hugged back just as firmly before helping her into the Hummer. Once they were seated, he held her eyes, pointed at the radio, and put a finger to his lips. She nodded firmly, and they drove in silence for several minutes until Buck pulled into the gravel parking lot of Barbecue Ranch, a vast log cabin with the bust of a pig peeking out from behind the chimney. He didn't speak until they were on the ground and had shut the doors of the Hummer.

"It's a serve-yourself buffet," he said. "Not fancy, but the tastiest barbecue around, and they use real coca in their hot chocolate."

"Sounds great!"

He offered his elbow and led her inside. "There's a table by the exit. Grab it before someone else does. What do you want?"

"A plate of barbecue chicken will be fine. Sweet

sauce, please."

"Got it. And I'll bring your hot chocolate, too."

Joz reached the table just before a couple about her age got there with filled trays—a table which, she thought with a sad smile, would allow Buck to eyeball everyone coming into the restaurant. *Just like Frank would.*

Expecting the couple to move on, she spotted Buck in line waiting to pay for their food.

"Excuse me, but we were planning to sit here."

Joz looked up. The female was slender, attractive, and had auburn hair. But she didn't sound friendly.

"I'm so sorry—my husband picks out the food," she said, thinking fast. "He's a veteran, always has to sit near a door. PTSD, you know."

"A vet, huh?" the man said, stepping forward. His shaved head made him look like an older Mr. Clean, though he was shorter and had a pot belly. "We'll squeeze into that booth in the corner, Mary."

"That's not fair, Joe," the woman named Mary said. "You're a veteran."

Joz, though feeling a lot better after the swim, felt her stomach tighten at the prospect of confrontation. She was still tense from the threat Buck identified and didn't need this woman trying to throw her weight around, especially when the man with her sounded reasonable. Had she been alone she might have moved, but this was the table Buck wanted. She stared daggers at the woman and crossed her arms over her chest.

"Mary," the man growled, "take the booth in the corner before we lose it…"

Buck stepped into view then and placed two trays loaded with food on the table. Joz reached for her hot chocolate and blew softly on it before smiling up at him—she was relieved he was back. She removed his canned Coca-Cola and set it aside his tray before Buck looked up at the couple.

"May I help you?"

"Your wife seems to think she deserves this table," Mary said. "My husband is also a veteran—"

Buck turned to him. "Soldier, that true?"

Joz hid a smile. He looked and sounded fierce, which seemed to put Mary on her heels for the moment.

"Yes, sir," Joe said. "Medic. Ninth Marine Regiment, Hamburger Hill."

"That was one hell of a skirmish."

"Yes, sir."

"At ease. No war going on now, and we're both retired."

Something in Buck's tone got Joz's attention. She took a discreet peek at him before settling into character as she had earlier. "Honey, remember what talking about the war does to you…"

"That's true, sugar." He moved to the empty seat next to the exit, which gave him a clear view of the entrance. Once next to Joz, he looked up and addressed the couple. "Please join us. I'm Buck. This is my wife, Jozelyn."

"I'm Joe," the man said, placing his tray on the table. He nodded to his wife, who reluctantly set her tray next to his. "My wife Mary."

"What do you two do?"

"We're both at the hospital," Joe said. "I'm an O.R. nurse. She's a receptionist."

"We're both overdue to retire, but Joe and I love helping people," Mary added. Joz felt the ice coming from her thaw a bit. "What about you guys?"

"She's an investor. Rental properties, mostly," Buck said. "I own a ranch about half an hour from town."

"Oh, one of those mini-farms everyone wants these days?"

"Hardly," Joz said while wiping sauce from her fingers. "Buck raises horses, and I can't keep track of our acreage. This man won't stop buying land."

"You own, what? Fifty acres? Or more?" Mary asked.

"Sometimes I wish we had something smaller so it would be less work for Buck. But horses need to roam and build muscle—essential for breeding well. To answer your question, fifteen *hundred* acres."

Mary choked on her food, and Joe had to whack her back to ease her momentary distress. Joz hid a smile but almost laughed when Buck kneed her under the table.

"Take a drink, Mary, if you're finished with your nosiness," Joe muttered.

"Joe, I was just—" She coughed into her napkin. "—making conversation."

Joe was describing his nursing position to Buck when Joz spotted two Asian men enter the food line. She gasped softly and an electric current of fear zipped through her. She squeezed Buck's forearm as discreetly as she could and chinned toward the front of the restaurant.

"Excuse me, Joe," Buck said quietly. "There may be some trouble afoot. I'm not crazy about a couple of people who just walked in."

Joe didn't turn to look over his shoulder. He leaned forward, and Joz felt his body language change. "You aren't fully retired, are you, sir? Anything I can do? I'm offering."

Joz, listening, was struck by how engrossed Mary was in handling a dripping rib. Was she totally oblivious and ignorant, or was she, too, playing some sort of role in this frightening drama?

"There's a black Suburban behind us, if you can see it out the window, Joe," Buck said softly. "It's parked close to my Hummer."

"I see it."

"I need that car not to run."

Joe stood, military bearing now on display. "On it, sir. Mary, don't steal my fries while I'm gone."

"Please. Anything I need to know, dear?" she asked, looking up while forking in a bite of coleslaw.

"Nope. Enjoy your lunch." Joe strode off toward the front of the restaurant. Joz watched him keep well away from the Asian men before reaching the front doors. Seconds later she heard footsteps on the gravel outside and saw the very top of Joe's head for an instant as he ducked beneath the window near them.

"He's underneath the Suburban," Buck said just loudly enough for Joz to hear. Mary was still wrapped up in her food and wiped her fingers on a napkin. The three of them ate in silence—Joz was able to manage a bite of chicken—until Joe returned. Gone less than five minutes, he plopped back into his chair and grabbed a handful of fries.

"I worked up an appetite puncturing those tires and snipping those wires," he said with a little grin.

"Good work, soldier," Buck said. "Thank you."

"I need the ladies' room," Joz said urgently.

"Hurry, sweetheart."

The bathrooms were only a few steps away, and Joz

made it inside and into a stall without having a full-fledged panic attack. She settled on the toilet and peed for what seemed like an hour while forcing herself to breathe slowly and deeply.

Calm down. Buck will get you out of here.

Buck was putting what was left of her meal in a Styrofoam to-go box when she returned. He tightened the lid on her hot chocolate and stood when he saw her. He looked all business, and she felt her stomach tighten again.

"Joe, Mary, it's been a pleasure," he said to the couple.

Joe stood. "The honor is mine, sir."

Mary simply nodded at them, her mouth filled with pork and sauce smeared on her chin. Buck moved to the exit door, and Joe came around to take his seat. Now he was across from Mary. Buck shoved open the door, nudged Joz outside and followed, then threw the door shut. She'd never been so glad to breathe frigid air as they jogged to the hummer.

****

"Are you kidding me?" Mary yelled through her mouthful of food. "You can't even sit next to me?"

Joe stood, blocking the Asian men from reaching them, and faced Mary. "Not now, okay? Maybe we need a break."

Baring her teeth, she rose and grabbed a heavy glass sugar shaker from the table and reared back. "I'll show you a break, Joe…"

Mary threw it wide of Joe—and directly into the forehead of the Asian man closest to them. Immediately bleeding, the man spouted a string of curses in broken English.

"What did you call my wife, sir?" Joe said loudly.

The first man lunged, blood dripping from his forehead, but Joe whirled and kicked him in the knee. The second man grabbed Joe's collar and tried to throw him aside, but Joe jabbed him in the throat with a quick right and kneed him in the groin, sending him to the floor. The first man dug in his waistband for a weapon when Joe grabbed a chair and slammed it on his head. Patrons were screaming and streaming out the front doors, but some of the commotion ceased when Mary announced loudly that she and Joe were with Border Patrol after cuffing the two attackers.

****

"Knowing Joe and Mary like I do—which aren't their real names—it'll be like them to make off with the weapons they grab off those commie bastards before they're arrested," he said. "Those guys were amateurs, for which I'm thankful."

Joz took the hot chocolate cup with shaking hands. "You did know them. I thought you behaved too friendly under the circumstances."

"How 'bout we get out of here, sugar-babe." Buck laughed as the hummer sped down the road.

"That was *much* too close for comfort."

Chapter Twenty-Seven

The restaurant was several miles in the rearview mirror. Only now was Joz beginning to relax. Buck, hitting a straightaway on a lonesome two-lane highway surrounded by bleak pastureland and the occasional leafless tree, yanked the radio from his dashboard and inspected it while keeping one eye on the road. He grunted as he spotted a bug behind the unit and pointed it out to Joz before lowering his window. She shivered as a blast of cold air hit her and was startled when he tossed the unit into the highway. She turned in time to see it explode into pieces on the asphalt. Not another vehicle was in sight.

"Well, Joz. That was a piece of cake," he said after raising the window.

This irritated her. She slurped her now-lukewarm hot chocolate, capped the drink, and put it in the cupholder before turning to Buck. "I don't know how you can laugh at what happened back there. Mary was obnoxious enough without the enemy walking in. I don't know who I liked less: her, or those spies."

"Operatives, little lady, not spies. And in case you haven't figured it out, the agency sent Joe and Mary, our guardian angels—" Buck grinned at her. "—*Joseph* and Mary. Get it?"

Joz rolled her eyes, not in the mood. "I wanted to

smack her."

"I'm glad you didn't. She's known for her short temper and fast moves." He slapped her knee lightly. "I know you were scared, and you handled yourself well. I'm proud of you."

"Well, thanks," she said, softening a bit. Then she frowned. "Hey, this isn't the way home…"

He said nothing.

"Buck?"

"We aren't going home, Joz. We're headed for Canada, specifically Calgary. We'll catch a flight to London because we need information on Frank. I'm sure there's paperwork to sign."

"Paperwork in England? What—why?"

"The agency assumes Frank is dead, but without a body there's no proof. He loved you more than life itself and left you everything, but that means paperwork and your signature to collect."

"*Loves* me, Buck, not past tense. But I'll play along: what did he leave me?"

"The St. Croix mansion, investments, and cash. Not to mention he died in action. That entitles you to a healthy stipend from the British government and insurance money. Then there's his trust fund, and we have no idea what's in his safe deposit box. All of which, Jozelyn Hardt, makes you a very wealthy woman."

She looked out the window at the bleak conditions while thinking this over. The St. Croix home had to be worth a couple million, and Frank had funds he'd told her he banked over the years.

"Frank—" She caught herself just in time. "—*is* a very generous man, Buck. We certainly agree on that, as well as the fact that he *loves* me with all his heart. But unlike you, I refuse to believe he's dead—"

"You might want to get involved in some philanthropy work."

Joz's temper flared. "Oh, that's a dandy idea. I could clean the oceans and mentor kids in the orphanages… or I could hire some enterprising soul to find Frank for me. Then I could refund everything to him."

Buck didn't respond, and they drove in silence. Joz was briefly transfixed by several horses sprinting through a clearing before disappearing into a stand of barren trees. The sight of the sleek brown animals against the white conditions would make a great watercolor.

"I know it's much too soon to talk about your inheritance," Buck said. "We'll do that when you're ready. No hurry."

"Look, I don't mean to be short with you. But all I want is Frank. I'd live a pauper's life to be with him. Frank Loveland makes me emotionally wealthy. That's the kind of wealth I want. Without him, the money isn't worth a nickel, far as I'm concerned."

The first car they'd seen in some time came from the other direction and blew past them as if on the Autobahn. Buck spoke once the road was theirs again.

"The kind of love you're describing comes along once in a lifetime, Joz. I understand that." He turned to her. "But if Frank does live, he won't know who you are anymore. That's not what you want to hear, but it isn't up for debate—it just *is*. Try to let that sink in, okay?"

She looked out the window again, almost wishing she could jump from it. Her mind wouldn't accept the prospect that a living, breathing Frank in the same excellent physical condition as when they'd parted would have no idea who she was.

"Besides, other kinds of relationships work just fine," Buck added.

"What relationships? What on earth are you talking about?"

"The friend's love works well. I'm talking about having each other's back, completely trusting your partner. It might not be sexually and emotionally intense, but it's solid and true."

Joz's mouth fell open. There was no mistaking what Buck was getting at.

She'd been aware for some time that he felt something for her. But he'd told her he absolutely swore to Frank that he would *not* pursue a relationship with his best friend's wife while watching over her at his Montana ranch.

Oh, God, how do I handle this? "I must know about Frank before I can think about anything else. Okay?"

"Of course," Buck said quietly.

Joz shifted in her seat, close to telling him to pull over so she could locate her inhaler. "Remember, it was you that said I'm empathic. I would have *felt* it if he'd been killed." She took a deep breath, trying to gather her thoughts. "I appreciate your friendship and honestly more than you know—"

"If the worst has happened, I'll wait until you're ready to move on. As long as it takes."

"Buck…"

"I needed to say all that—get it off my chest."

"Please look at me."

He checked the road, then turned to her with fear in his eyes. He was bracing for bad news, she was certain.

"Promise me you'll find out what happened to him. I mean, *really* find out."

"I'll find out, Joz. I swear on everything holy."

****

They reached the Canadian border before sunset. Buck lowered his window and handed their passports to a tall, stern-looking uniformed officer with an intimidating hat. The man looked them over without changing expression.

"Mr. and Mrs. Bigelow?"

"That's us," Buck said.

"Purpose of visiting Canada?"

Joz took an immediate dislike to the man. *None of your damned business.*

"My bride has never been. We thought we'd take an extended drive, see the sights. It's a beautiful country."

The officer finally smiled a bit. "Very good, sir. I hope you enjoy Canada, Mrs. Bigelow."

"Uh, thank you, Officer."

"You may proceed, Mr. Bigelow. Be safe, sir."

The bleak wilderness on the Canadian side looked just like it had on the American side, but Joz felt her heart lighten.

"I'm in Canada, Buck! Tell me the truth... are we really traveling?"

"We're headed to the airport, but we could explore after we return," Buck said. "Julio will watch the ranch for months—"

"Months?"

"—yes, Joz. Before Dabney died, he wanted to move his family to Montana. I bet he'd be up for staying a while."

Joz said nothing. Her home, when you got down to it, was the ranch back in Montana. But they were going to London to sign paperwork deeding everything Sir

Frank Loveland owned over to her. But what was she going to do all day for *months* while Buck tried to get to the bottom of Frank's disappearance, and where were they going to stay if crazy, vengeful killers were after them? Did she even have a home anymore? She pictured Cammy in her mind and wondered what her friend would suggest she do.

This time Cammy didn't have an answer.

****

George sat in his office at agency headquarters rubbing his forehead with his left hand and clenching the phone with his right. Waiting for the Prime Minister to pick up was frustrating, and it wasn't like he could mouth off to him when he did.

"Yes, George. What is it?"

"Sir, I must report unfortunate information." George heaved a sigh. "Frank Loveland didn't make it. He drowned off the Swiss coast after his boat exploded while being chased by us and the Chinese nationals."

"What would cause a boat to explode like that?"

"Automatic gunfire hitting the gas tank directly, or the extra fuel he carried on board. Frank ran over a well-hidden reef, which caused a gaping hole in the bow. Anyway, sir, I assure you the counterfeit money fed the fire before the boat sank into the depths—Chinese nationalists watched the entire event. No worries about the evidence against England, but with Frank, it is a bloody awful business."

"Wasn't Frank one of our greatest operatives?"

George sighed again. "Yes, in his day. But he was nearing seventy and rusty at fieldwork. He knew it might be a one-way street and prepared a will for his wife. England shall take excellent care of his American bride."

"I'd like to send her my condolences. Where is Mrs. Loveland?"

"I expect her any time. A former agent named Buck Bigelow has been looking after her, and he called to say they were waiting on the Calgary-to-London redeye. They should land soon."

Chapter Twenty-Eight

"We haven't been flying an hour, and we hit bumpy weather already?" Joz asked when she felt the doors above them rattle. "This makes me nervous."

"Don't worry," Buck said. "The captain said we'll be through it soon."

Joz closed her eyes again and thought about Frank. Under normal circumstances she would have been delighted to tour England. But under normal circumstances she'd be sitting next to Frank, not Buck.

"Thinking about Frank?"

Her eyes snapped open. *Do you live in my head now, Buck?*

"We hadn't talked about visiting his homeland, and it's a little bittersweet to go without him."

"I understand."

"No, you don't," she said, irritated now. "No offense, Buck—I'm grateful for your company and protection, but fully grasping that he won't know me won't happen overnight. Please try to understand that."

"I will. And we're about halfway there. Let's get some shut-eye."

That's the best idea you've had all day. She reclined her seat back and hugged a small pillow, drifting off almost immediately. In her dreams, she and Frank danced to a lovely Peter Maren melody the superstar crooned in Spanish. Frank interpreted the words and sang them as they swayed to the music.

You are my life... my heart... my love...

Frank was blurry when she pulled away from him after the dance, and she realized both had tears in their eyes. Suddenly they were being transported to a hospital. Frank reached out for her, but she floated away.

My love... stay with me...

"Ladies and gentlemen, I'm Captain Williams," a deep male voice boomed.

"Expect a brisk morning in London but with clear skies. Place your seats in the upright, locked position and prepare for landing. Thank you for choosing British Air."

Joz blinked several times and sat up. "We're about to land. I hate this part."

Buck put his arm around her and pulled her close. "Don't worry, little lady. I've got you. This will be over soon."

She closed her eyes and burrowed into his chest. She was aware of him stroking her hair, which made her feel safe and protected as the minutes passed and the plane descended.

"Good, we're down," Buck said a few minutes later after a low thump, followed by a smaller one. "Now for a nice, smooth—"

BANG!

Joz was thrown to her left before being hurled back into Buck's arms when the plane jerked one way, then the other. The seatbelt had kept her in her seat, but terror surged through her as passengers began screaming. Fully awake now, she knew this was no dream. The plane was on the ground but still moving swiftly and careening out of control. She knew in her bones they were in serious trouble.

Please God, protect us. I love you, Frank.

"A tire blew," Buck said. "Lean forward, Joz. Put your head down. I've got you. I love you, Joz."

"We're going to crash, aren't we?"

He didn't answer. Waiting until the last possible moment, he unbuckled his seatbelt and hers. He set her on the floor of the food preparation alcove situated ahead of their seats, a small space that extended across the aisle. Her eyes closed tightly; she felt Buck crouch over the top of her. She wondered why he didn't throw himself directly on top of her. Wasn't he leaving himself exposed if—

BOOM!

****

"Head trauma. Order a CAT scan. *Stat.*"

"Yes, Doctor."

A nurse? What's happening?

"This patient needs surgery," came another voice.

"Too late for this one—he's gone."

Chapter Twenty-Nine

Joz awoke to an eerie silence. She looked around, frightened, and saw an IV drip hooked into her left arm. All at once she was cognizant of the pain in her head and throughout her body, though it felt dulled to a degree. She squinted, recognizing that a curtain was draped around her bed, but through a gap she saw what looked like white walls. Everything was blurry, and she felt herself begin to drift away.

"Time to wake up."

Stay with me.

Joz forced her eyes open. The male voice was familiar. She tried to sit up, really feeling the pain.

"Good morning, Mrs.—"

"Where am I?" She barely recognized her voice.

The doctor pointed a beam of light into her aching eyes. "Tell me what you remember."

"An accident?"

"Are you guessing or remembering?"

"I... I'm not sure," she murmured.

"You suffered a head injury, luv," the doctor said. "We made room for your brain swelling, and your situation was critical for a while. But fortune smiled upon you: no broken bones, no internal injuries. You're badly bruised, but those will heal. We'll monitor your brain and make sure it heals properly too."

"Okay…"

****

Joz had no idea how much time had passed when the doctor spoke again.

"Good morning."

This time it didn't hurt as much to sit up, though she was still groggy. He leaned in and aimed the little bead of light into her eyes. "Tell me your name."

"My name… I'm not sure…"

The doctor was in a white lab coat. He looked over his shoulder, and a nurse in pink scrubs stepped into view.

"Do you know what year it is?" she asked.

"Year? I… I don't know…"

"What's the name of the president of your country?"

"I… uh… my head hurts. Make it stop."

The doctor placed his hand on her arm, which calmed her. "The nurse will administer additional pain medication to make your head feel better. Memory loss occurs with this kind of injury—"

"It does?" Joz asked.

"—yes, and we found your name from documents. We shall allow the remaining memories to return naturally. Just be patient. You will be quite sore, but you fared well. I'll check with you later."

Joz heard the doctor order another scan before she drifted off again.

Come back to me.

****

"Hello, Mrs. Bigelow. How do you feel today?"

This was a female voice. Joz opened her eyes. "Where am I?" She cleared her throat and found it hard to swallow. "Why… why is my voice weak?"

"You are in Royal District Hospital recovering from surgery for a head injury. The doctor will be here shortly."

"My throat hurts."

"We intubated you whilst you were in an induced coma. But your doctors agree that it is time to bring you into reality."

Squinting, Joz saw that this nurse was an older woman. She sure was chipper and had a singsong voice that relaxed Joz.

"I've been asleep?" she said to the nurse.

The woman chuckled. "For weeks, dear. You have been through the wars but come through like a champion."

I was in a war?

A male doctor in a white lab coat hustled into the room. "Good morning, Mrs. Bigelow," he said, checking charts that hung at the edge of her bed. Was this a doctor she'd spoken to before? She couldn't recall. *And who is Bigelow?*

"Good morning," Joz said.

"How do you feel?

"Confused."

"That's quite normal. Can you tell me your name?"

"My name? Well... I can't remember, except you call me Bigelow... such an odd name."

Neither the doctor nor the nurse with the singsong voice changed expression.

"Everything seems fine." He pointed the little beam of light into her eyes. "The shock of waking in a hospital should wear off, and your memories will resurface. Meanwhile, Mrs. Bigelow, a specialist will visit with you. Pending her report, you may be released soon. If you think of any questions, please tell the nurse."

He nodded at the nurse and strode from the room. Watching him leave, Joz noticed a bouquet of wilted, yellow roses that sat on her nightstand.

"Who sent those?"

"Let's see," the nurse said, stepping over to them. "The tag is smudged. The room number appears but the sender's initials look like P.M. You've a mystery admirer, Mrs. Bigelow." Her smile faded. "Something wrong, dear?"

"You're British. The doctor is British. Could I be in England?"

The nurse smiled again. "This hospital is in London, but I would prefer Dr. Ahmed answer your questions. She should step through the door any minute."

"Do I live in London?"

"Hello, my name is Dr. Ahmed," a short, trim female announced, bursting into the room with a clipboard in hand. She, too, had an English accent, and pulled over a chair.

"Can you tell me your name?"

"Everyone wants my name," Joz said.

"No pressure—we just want to help."

"My name… I'm clueless. How odd." Joz focused on the doctor, who was energetic and seemed like a nice person. "Will you explain what happened to me?"

Dr. Ahmed took her hand. "You survived a plane crash. But your brain swelled, and bleeding on the brain followed. Doctors removed a small portion of your skull to relieve the pressure and then worked to fix the bleeding, inducing a coma. Sometimes after a person's body experiences all that trauma, it affects the memory. I assure you it will return—forcing it won't help."

"Doctor, Mrs. Bigelow doesn't remember London and is concerned."

"Thank you, Nurse Jennifer," Dr. Ahmed said over her shoulder before meeting Joz's gaze again. "You must feel out of sorts. I am guessing you own no house or flat where you can heal?"

"I have… no idea. How could I know?"

"I see. You have excellent coverage, and the airline covers everything insurance does not. We shall place you in family quarters. Doctors will discharge you tomorrow if you feel well enough." Dr. Ahmed stood. "Let's help you from bed and prepare you to walk."

"I'll use a walker?" Joz asked, spotting one by her bed.

"Until you feel strong enough to walk without it," the nurse said. She adjusted the bed to an upright position and lowered it, and Joz sat up straight for the first time in what apparently had been weeks. Seeing the room from a normal position oriented her senses. "Now, swing your legs over the side… good… feeling dizzy?"

"No," Joz said sharply. "That floor is freezing. And I'm hungry."

"Let's put these on," the nurse said, slipping socks with treads on the bottom onto Joz's feet. "And it is good to hear you have an appetite."

"Yes," Dr. Ahmed said. "Hunger indicates that your injuries are mending. After you stroll one stretch up the hallway and return with Nurse Jennifer, I shall send an order to the kitchen. Now… up you go, Mrs. Bigelow."

The doctor and nurse helped her to her feet, and the nurse put her hands over Joz's and squeezed them to the grips of the walker.

"How does that feel?" Nurse Jennifer asked.

"Everything is sore. Good grief."

"Your contusions covered your limbs and back. Considering their severity, I am not surprised they still pain you," Dr. Ahmed said. "How does it feel to stand? Do you think you can make it up and down the hall?"

"I'd sure like to try," Joz said.

She managed to reach the doorway then into the hall, mumbling to the nurse that her muscles felt as wobbly as a toddler's.

"That's quite normal," Nurse Jennifer said. "Carefully, now… one foot in front of the other. You have much better balance than I would have imagined. Your legs look strong—do you feel okay?"

"Just like I did five steps ago. Hungry and weak."

"If I know Dr. Ahmed," Nurse Jennifer said, "food will be waiting in your room by the time you return, dear."

"That's good motivation," Joz said, pushing herself forward. The hallway smelled of ammonia. Doctors and nurses seemed to be everywhere, and all seemed to be in a rush as they passed her. "I must look like a wreck—everyone is staring at me."

Nurse Jennifer patted her arm. "You look like someone who was in a coma."

It's frightening having everyone ogling. "Is my behind sticking out?"

"Your gown covers amply, Mrs. Bigelow."

They continued until the hallway split in two directions. Joz paused, catching her breath as she looked in one direction and then the other.

"You walk ably," Nurse Jennifer said. "Shall we return to your room?"

"Yes. I'm tired, but I'll make it."

Dr. Ahmed was waiting as Joz settled into bed. "Did anyone mention that your head was shaved so surgeons could insert a plate? That may account for some staring, but don't worry—some down is beginning to grow."

"Well, that's one mystery solved," Joz mumbled. She reached up to touch the peach fuzz that was growing in patches on her scalp. "No wonder everyone gawked."

"Mrs. Bigelow, few women carry off the hairless style, but you look quite fetching."

Joz laughed, which made her throat hurt. "Sure, for a bald woman, Doctor."

"You might want to wear a hat or scarf. The gift shop provides a lovely selection. Shall I have them send a few to you?"

"That would be fine, thank you. And my clothes?"

"Jennifer, take a look, please?"

The nurse opened the closet, flipped on a light, then backed out with a frown on her face. "Oh, my… there's a winter coat and cowgirl boots. Nothing else."

Cowgirl Boots? What is wrong with me? Why can't I remember?

"The nurses cut everything off after you arrived in the emergency room," the nurse added. "And the gift shop doesn't carry clothes except for t-shirts."

"Ah, your food has arrived," Dr. Ahmed said as a male orderly rolled a cart into the room and up to the bed. "I shall leave you to it and visit later."

Joz watched Dr. Ahmed hustle out. The orderly smiled but said nothing, wheeling the cart out of the room once Nurse Jennifer had placed the tray where Joz could reach it easily.

"What is this stuff?"

"Remember, you have had a feeding tube for weeks,

Mrs. Bigelow. You must begin with liquids to reacclimate to solids. How about starting with the broth?"

Joz blew on it, tried a bite, and made a face. "Blech. This is dishwater."

"Maybe the Jell-O will be more palatable."

The Jell-O was in a container, which Joz was able to open without asking for help. The mold was red, but she smiled after forking a small bite into her mouth.

"Cherry—not bad. I could eat two or three of these."

"Easy does it," Nurse Jennifer said. "Lunch will be served in a couple of hours. I'll make certain the kitchen delivers a duplicate meal with extra Jell-O."

"I'd rather have French fries."

"Doctor's orders, Mrs. Bigelow."

"I'm kidding. May I take a shower?"

"It would probably do you a world of good. Just be gentle with your head."

The nurse fished a fresh gown from the closet and told Joz to take the walker into the shower.

"Pull the cord if you experience any difficulties," she said. "And we appear to be of similar size, Mrs. Bigelow. I shall gift you a proper sweater and a pair of jeans. You must leave the hospital in something warm and appropriate."

"Thank you, Jennifer. Would you mind getting me a new pair of panties?"

"I'll be glad to, dear."

Once in the shower, Joz let the warm water flow over her head and felt no pain to speak of as she massaged shampoo onto her scalp. She dispensed soap and took a good look at her legs—there was a faint outline of bruising on them—mild pain persisted as she washed herself from top to bottom. She buff-dried herself with a towel and slipped into the fresh gown and socks that hung on the door. Then she rubbed the fog from the mirror and dared to look.

Who are you, woman? How did you get here? Oh, my, you need sunshine. You look like a raccoon's ghost.

She pushed her walker out of her room and moved slowly toward the sunlight at the end of the hallway, where she found a padded bench. She got herself seated and felt warmed by the sunbeam, which lifted her spirits. Looking out the window, she saw a red double-decker bus passing on the narrow street below. Suddenly she felt exhausted. She stretched out on the bench, found it warm and reassuring, and closed her eyes.

Chapter Thirty

"Mrs. Bigelow, there you are," an unfamiliar female voice barked, rousing Joz from a dream that disappeared into nothingness before she could remember any of it. She was still on the padded bench at the end of the hall, the sun still warm on her. "I've been searching for you. It's lunchtime—let's go."

Without warning the woman—a nurse, apparently—pulled her arm and dragged her up into a sitting position. When it looked like the nurse was going to pull her to her feet, Joz shoved her hands away.

"Just a second, please. I was sound asleep."

The nurse, who was short and heavy with graying hair in a tight bun, looked offended and mumbled something Joz couldn't make out.

"Excuse me?"

"You must stand and return to your room—right now. This seating is for visitors, not patients."

"I don't think I got your name…"

"I'm Nurse Constance." The woman started to reach for Joz's arm, but Joz, pushing to her feet, stepped back and grabbed her walker.

"I can walk on my own, thank you. Where's Jennifer?"

"As I was about to say, things run on a tight schedule around here, Mrs. Bigelow, and I don't lose patients the way Jennifer does."

"She didn't lose me—I'm right in front of you," Joz snapped before starting forward with her walker. "And there's no need for you to hold my arm. I'm not an invalid. I'll walk out of this hospital tomorrow, totally alone."

"Oh? I didn't see that on your chart."

Joz didn't acknowledge the comment and left the woman standing there. Lunch was indeed waiting by her bed—it was a repeat of the broth with two dessert containers this time. Getting herself back into bed and adjusting it to be able to eat sitting up, she ignored the broth but swiftly downed the first container of Jell-O while enjoying the lemon-flavored tea.

"Ooh," she said after opening the second container. "Crème Brulé?"

Smiling from ear to ear, she closed her eyes and savored the first bite. She couldn't remember the last time she'd had the delicious dessert.

"Who gave you that?" Nurse Constance asked harshly.

Joz opened her eyes. The ugly little woman was four feet away, having crept in without a sound. "It came on the tray. What business of it is yours?"

"This hospital does *not* serve that pudding. Give it to me."

Replacing the top on the container before Constance could grab it, Joz hugged it to her chest. "Over my dead body are you getting it. Now, *vamoose* before I call your superior. Jennifer is my nurse, not you."

"You can bet I'll check with culinary about this." Constance reached over and grabbed the spoon before Joz could reach it, then stormed from the room.

You better eat this before that witch returns.

She yanked open the container and used her finger to eat, gobbling the dessert as if her life depended on it. She was finishing the container when she heard two steps of footsteps coming back down the hall. Nurse Constance, huffing and puffing as if she'd sprinted up several flights of stairs, arrived just ahead of a much taller, older woman who struck Joz as warm, friendly—and calm.

"Mrs. Bigelow, we usually take better care of our patients and only allow them hospital foods," she said sweetly.

"I understand, but the pudding was sealed, and God bless the kind soul who gave it to me. I appreciate it more than you know."

Constance, after glaring at Joz, turned to her supervisor. "And what are we going to do about this?"

"We've more important things to worry about on this floor. I don't expect you to bother me again about something so trite, Constance."

It took everything Joz had to keep from bursting into laughter.

"Trite?" Constance spluttered. "Well, I never…"

"You heard Mrs. Bigelow—the container was sealed. Now please get back to work. This patient is under the care of Jennifer."

"Americans." Constance spun on her heel and marched out of the room.

"I apologize, Mrs. Bigelow." The supervisor extended her hand. "I'm Bella. You've experienced enough hardship to enjoy a crème brulé from whomever brought it. Push the call button and ask for me if Nurse Constance gives you any trouble."

"I will. Thank you, Bella."

"Oh, and your chart indicates amnesia, yet you remembered Crème Brule?"

Joz nodded firmly. "I sure did. Why would I remember a favorite dessert and so little else? Does that mean I'm recovering?"

"That is not my area of expertise, but I shall note it on the chart for Dr. Ahmed. She'll certainly want to know. As to you leaving here tomorrow, orderlies will transfer you to the visitor's building. It is quite small but comfortable and will provide easy access to your counselor—she'll work with you on your memory. Also, you have an appointment to see the neurosurgeon in a couple of days."

"Okay. How long will I be in a visitor's room?"

"Dr. Ahmed will make that call. Just try to be patient."

A patient patient. Joz began to giggle.

****

Late that afternoon Joz was napping when she thought she heard someone in the room. Opening one eye, she saw it was Nurse Jennifer, who had clothes in her arms. Joz shut her eye before Jennifer looked her way, and Joz heard her enter the closet. She waited until the kind nurse had left the room and closed the door, then eased out of bed and walked over to the closet to look inside.

Jennifer had left her a new sweater, new jeans, and new panties. Joz smiled and got back in bed to nap some more.

Chapter Thirty-One

Joz studied her first-floor quarters, which contained a bed, dresser, and a TV set. Cheap prints of outdoor scenes hung on white walls. A lone chair sat by a window with a view of the courtyard next to the hospital. The courtyard was a nice thing for families of patients, and the room had been dusted and smelled clean.

"What's this?" she asked aloud in the quiet. A large box was in the corner with MR. BIGELOW written in black ink on top. The box wasn't taped shut, and Joz discovered items that belonged to her late husband: a winter coat, credit cards in both their names, her passport, and rings in a plastic baggie she quickly tried on. To her amazement, they barely stayed on her fingers. She put them back in the baggie, thinking she might need to make crème brulé a regular part of her diet for at least a few days.

"My dear husband, whoever you were, it breaks my heart that I can't remember you. You must have had some money. This is *fine* jewelry."

As Joz sifted through the man's belongings she felt a profound loss and a surprisingly strong sense of guilt. She narrowed her eyes in concentration as she noticed a typed report at the bottom of the box. Removing it carefully, she felt her breath catch when she saw it was filled out by the medic at the crash scene.

She sat down on the bed to read it. "My husband gave his life for mine," she said aloud. Biting her lip to hold back tears, she set the report aside and grabbed a boot from the box. She held it to her nose and inhaled deeply.

"Smells like leather… and *horse*? Weird."

She put the boot back, then grabbed his large winter coat and stood, holding it in front of her. Her husband had been a big, powerful man, based on the length and width of his coat. She tossed her leather coat aside and slipped into the much larger and heavier garment that felt great in the chilly room. She stuffed her hands in the pockets to warm them and felt a tag. She pulled it out and peered at it.

"Harrod's Fine Clothing," she said aloud. "Maybe that's where I should shop tomorrow. I'll certainly need a new wardrobe and hat for nippy London."

****

She slept well enough but still felt low on energy after eating the breakfast that was brought to her: a bowl of broth, Jell-O, and a banana. She showered and dressed, then rewrapped her scarf, put on her leather coat, grabbed her walker, and stepped outside to hail a taxi. To her surprise, a Mercedes pulled up almost immediately. A handsome young man in a suit popped out of the luxury car, opened the passenger door, then made sure she was situated before folding her walker and storing it in the trunk.

"Where to, miss?" he asked politely after pulling into traffic.

"Is a store called Harrod's nearby?"

"Certainly is. Not far at all."

Winded after all the moving around in the last few

minutes, Joz closed her eyes and sat still for several minutes before a thought occurred to her.

"I'm carrying American bills," she said to the driver. "I hope that isn't a problem. Do you take credit cards?"

"This ride is on the house. We're happy to accommodate our American friends."

"Are you sure? I'll also need a ride back too."

"Both rides will be free of charge. It is no problem at all, miss."

The driver zipped through traffic, taking a bit of a chance as he went through an impending red light at a busy intersection. Then he hit his blinker and swerved into the far left most lane before easing to a stop.

"Here we are," he said. "Let me get your walker."

Joz's eyes widened at the sheer size of Harrod's, which loomed in front of her. The driver hit the trunk release and hopped out of the car. She opened her door, felt a blast of frigid air, and smiled when the driver offered his hand to help her to her feet. He opened the walker and set it before her, then reached inside his jacket and handed her a business card that read SURVEILLANCE, INC.

"Call me when you're ready to go back," he said.

"I will, but I absolutely insist on paying you…"

"I assure you there's no need, miss. Enjoy your shopping."

The driver jumped back into the Mercedes and merged into traffic before a flood of vehicles came down the street. Joz watched his car disappear, then turned to Harrod's, trying to take it in. The department store rose from the ground like a mountain. Really feeling tired now with the London winter boring into her, she hobbled on her walker toward the double front doors.

A doorman opened the entryway as she approached and welcomed her, then pointed past a jewelry counter when she asked for the women's section. A young saleswoman approached instantly and asked how she could be of help.

"This is my first visit to your beautiful store." Joz leaned on her walker for support as she caught her breath. "I need casual clothes and lingerie."

"Your first time? Your coat is from one of our top designers."

"You know, maybe I have been here before." Joz caught the woman's suspicion and smiled apologetically. "I'm sorry. I was in an accident, and my memory—"

"Ah, no need to apologize, madame. And your timing is marvelous! Let's go to the second floor, and I'll grab an attendant who knows our merchandise better than everyone here. He is in a meeting that should wrap up any minute; he will be glad to assist you."

They took an escalator, the clerk handling the walker for Joz as they climbed. She set it in front of Joz once they stepped out onto the second floor.

"There are some comfortable chairs right over there," the clerk said, pointing. "I'll grab Tony and let him know you are waiting, then get you a cup of coffee if you would like to sit down."

"That would be wonderful," Joz murmured. "Cream only, please."

The woman returned with a steaming mug of coffee and said Tony would be with her in a few minutes. Joz thanked her, then leaned back in a comfy leather chair and felt it envelop her—she would conk right out if she wasn't careful. The coffee mug was hot but not scalding and felt great in her cold hands. She took slow deep breaths, reminding herself that she was pushing a lot harder this morning than anyone at the hospital would have preferred.

"Good morning! I am Tony. How may I help you this fine morning?"

Joz opened her eyes and set the coffee on an end table. Tony was tall and thin with curly brown hair, dressed in a stylish navy-blue suit. A pinstriped handkerchief adorned the breast pocket of the jacket.

"I'm Mrs. Bigelow. I was expecting—I take it you're familiar with women's clothing?"

"Oh, yes!" He clapped his hands. "I actually design female apparel. You let me know what you are looking for, and I shall find it."

"Well, practical clothing, but good quality... a couple of sweaters, couple of pairs of slacks, a dress or two, and a warm hat to match this coat. Oh, undergarments and some lingerie... I do need shoes... and a purse and a suitcase large enough to carry the items I'm purchasing today." She started to get up. "As I told the kind young lady, I suffer from at least temporary memory loss. I hope I'm not too much trouble..."

"Mrs. Bigelow, I was told about your memory—no trouble at all—keep your seat and relax, enjoy your coffee. Give me a bit to select clothes to match your lovely skin tone, and that suit your figure."

"It sounds like I'm in good hands, then. And Tony, the clothes I'm wearing were donated to me after the accident. All I own is this jacket and a pair of western boots."

Tony's smile stayed firmly in place. "Then we begin with a clean slate. I will say that you are much too attractive not to show yourself off—"

This made Joz blush so fiercely she could feel it in her cheeks.

"—I shall come back with several outfits that will look absolutely *smashing* on you. If you can try a couple of them on, I shall pick out the rest of your wardrobe for you and have it sent to your address. I am so certain of your complete satisfaction I will personally guarantee a full refund on all purchases if even *one* of them does not meet with your delight."

"All of that sounds wonderful, Tony. Thank you."

****

Tony was remarkably patient in the two hours he spent with Joz as she tried on several outfits, including two pairs of trousers she chose that fit too perfectly— after seeing her jewelry nearly fall off her fingers, she figured she was due to gain back a few pounds and would need a size larger tailored to her current size so she could let out the pants as needed. This triggered a memory she couldn't place…

Let them out. Let them out.

When she explained to Tony that her memory loss stemmed from the recent plane crash that killed three people, tears filled his eyes, and the gentle hand he put on her shoulder couldn't have seemed any more sincere and comforting. He even said he would hand-deliver her purchases to her room in the visitor's quarters of the hospital when she said she was staying there temporarily.

"Let me say again how wonderful it has been to serve you, Mrs. Bigelow," he said, standing alongside as another female rang up her purchases—Joz was spending well over two thousand dollars. "You have my card. If any item does not strike you as exactly right, you let me know and we shall arrange a return."

"Thank you so much," Joz said.

"Mrs. Bigelow, I shall see you this afternoon with your purchases. And if you have worked up an appetite, let me suggest the bistro on the first floor. It is crowded at lunch but still early enough that you could probably get a table."

Chapter Thirty-Two

Joz, comfortable in her new sweater and wool pants, maneuvered herself to the escalator and made it to the first floor of Harrod's while balancing the walker in front of her. As she drifted slowly downward, she had an almost majestic view of shoppers bustling about, many carrying large bags with purchases inside. Tony had told her to turn right once she came off the escalator to start toward the bistro, and she found it without having to ask directions. She was greeted by a young hostess who asked if she was meeting anyone.

"No, just me," Joz said.

"Right this way," the hostess directed, moving quickly and frowning when Joz had a hard time keeping up. She seated Joz at a table for two with a window overlooking a busy street. Joz propped her walker against the empty chair opposite her, draped her coat over it, and was watching the people outside when a laminated menu landed on the table with a *thunk.*

"You're not expecting anyone…?"

Startled, Joz looked up. A woman her age who didn't look terribly friendly was placing a glass of water in front of her.

"No. Will that be a problem?"

"What can I get for you?"

Though the hospital staff wanted her on liquids, she

197

didn't think a couple of French fries would hurt.

"How is the shrimp bisque?" she asked.

"Delicious," the woman said tonelessly. "Cup or bowl? Comes with French bread."

"A cup. And French Fries, please?"

"We call them *chips*. To drink?"

Joz took a long look at the woman. *See if I leave you a tip.* "Water is fine."

The woman took the menu without so much as a nod and started away. As she'd ordered, Joz was aware of a couple taking the table next to her. The woman caught her attention first: tall and heavy with bleached hair that was swept into an old-fashioned French twist. She wore so much jewelry Joz had to keep from staring at the substantial diamond studs, a diamond bracelet, and rings with colorful gems.

"Darling, I shall order for you," she said in a lilting voice that didn't match her build. "We will return you to excellent health."

Joz watched the man remove his overcoat. He had white hair that fell almost to his shoulders and a thick white beard and mustache, but this barely registered—both of his arms were covered with nasty scars. When she saw additional scars above his beard and eyebrows, she knew he'd been badly burned.

That could have been me. I hope my husband didn't suffer like that.

The same waitress came out to take their orders and, to Joz's great irritation, was friendly with them, almost charming. The silent treatment toward Joz continued when her own food was ready (the woman simply placed Joz's plate in front of her), but she focused instead on how good the bisque was. She couldn't help a smile when she dunked a French fry, enjoying the salty snack. She was finishing her soup when the couple's food was brought to them: a croissant loaded with shrimp and a bowl of almost clear liquid that made her think of hospital food. The woman pushed the bowl closer to the man.

He's eating broth. Isn't that a coincidence?

The woman was poised to take her first bite when her cell phone chirped. She groaned, looked at the screen, and said it was the jewelry department. After taking the call she promised the man across from her she'd be right back. Joz, trying to be discreet, watched her hurry away. It took a second before she realized the man was watching her.

"Isn't it a lovely day?" he asked.

"Cold, but yes, it's beautiful. I'm surprised. Shouldn't it be foggy?" Joz asked, then frowned. *Do I remember something associated with fog?*

"You're American, I take it?"

The man had a nice smile. "Yes... I think so."

"You *think* so?"

"Head injury, I'm afraid. No memory."

"Did a mishap occur in London?"

"Yes, at the airport—a plane crash last month. I'm told I was on it."

"I heard about it," he said. "But you made it through, didn't you?"

"Thanks to a husband I can't remember and excellent doctors, yes."

"May I be so bold to ask what your doctors say about your memory loss?" he asked.

"They believe it's temporary—I'm sure hoping so. My outpatient checkup is today. Do you work in the medical field, sir?"

"I don't. I experienced memory loss, too, partly from the fire. But it certainly isn't as all-encompassing as yours."

"Believe me, it's no fun not knowing my name or where I belong," she said.

"I can only imagine. You reside in London?"

"My passport says Montana, in the States. But I'm staying at the family center attached to Royal District Hospital until they help me remember."

The man nodded firmly. "That's a renowned clinic. They specialize in neurology and neurosurgery, so you are in exceptional hands." He smiled again and extended his arms, which she thought was brave. "As you see, I have been through the wars."

Someone said that to me—Nurse Jennifer! "Do you hurt?"

"A bit when nurses work on the scarring. Queen Victoria Hospital specializes in burns like mine. We are both lucky to be on this earth."

Something about the man's kindness and gentleness tugged at Joz's heart. She really liked his smile, and his eyes were kind and soft.

"I'm not trying to be rude—you're with your wife?" she asked softly.

The man smiled, but Joz couldn't read this one. "She says so, but I cannot remember. Rose found me strolling nearby and claimed she knew me as her husband from years ago. She produced photos that proved we were once married."

"Then she's the fortunate one. I wish my husband were alive."

"He was also on the plane?"

"Yes. I learned that he moved me from our assigned seats before we collided with the parked jet. He saved my life—the crash destroyed our seat section."

"What a gentleman, thinking of your safety. A real hero."

"Yes, I suppose so." Joz gazed out at the crowded London street. She felt an odd mix of emotions: grief bordering on despair at losing a man who must have been devoted to her, and grateful for someone (or something) she couldn't recall.

"Please accept my apology," the man said. "I upset you."

She faced him and shook her head. "It isn't that. I'm feeling emotions I can't put into words. That frustrates me so much."

The man lowered his voice. "Oh, I understand. This Rose woman insists we were married, and maybe we were... but it couldn't have been an attachment that involved my heart."

Joz wasn't sure how to respond. Her husband had died in the plane crash—that was demonstrably true—but what if he'd survived somehow? *Would she remember him?* How awful would it be not to recognize him, or anything about him. She couldn't imagine.

"Please forgive me for saying this," the man continued, "but for some reason I'm absolutely entranced by your eyes. In fact, they cause me to wonder about this grief—which I must admit has lifted a bit since seeing them."

This made Joz blush nearly as much as Tony's compliment about her figure. "Oh, my," she managed. "Well, I probably shouldn't say this to a stranger, but your eyes make me feel comfortable. And I understand the deep sadness—when I awoke from the coma it was like I lost someone dear to me."

Rose returned and joined the man, promptly taking a huge bite of her croissant. He explained that he and Joz enjoyed a nice visit while she was away.

"We compared scars," he added.

The woman, her cheeks packed full, looked over at Joz and said nothing. She looked about as warm as a glacier.

"Hello." Joz smiled politely.

"I don't see any scars," she snapped while dabbing her mouth with a napkin.

"Head injury—memory loss."

The woman sighed, a dismissive sound. "He claims that, too."

"Amnesia is a frustrating thing," Joz said carefully, trying to watch her tone after taking an instant dislike to the woman. Nor did she want this kind man upset at her, a man who seemed so *familiar*. "But your husband has put me at ease over it. You must feel fortunate finding him again."

Rose finished chewing, swallowed, and wiped her mouth again before aiming an index finger at Joz. "Fortunate?" she barked, almost spitting the word. "My husband disappeared nine years ago and was declared dead. Now he returns, looking like a monstrous vagabond, and he didn't bother to contact me! I found him roaming the *streets*, my dear lady. I wouldn't say that's fortunate."

"At least your husband is alive," Joz snapped.

"And what good is that if he has no idea who I am?"

"Excuse me, but memory loss is not something anyone chooses, much less enjoys. I suggest you count your blessings instead of being such a selfish—"

Joz clapped a hand over her mouth before finishing the thought, but it was too late. Rose, who acted like she'd been slapped, glared at the long-haired man.

"I refuse to sit with this riffraff! We shall leave, right this minute."

"Rose," he said calmly, "I am not going anywhere."

Joz's heart fluttered at the quiet power of the man's words. She could almost feel a memory, or *something*...

"Suit yourself," Rose said flippantly. She thrust herself to her feet and nearly overturned her chair. "Frankly, *luv*, I wish you had never returned. I truly wish you were dead."

Joz's mouth fell open. But the man said nothing, and if his body language meant anything, he struck Joz as relieved. Rose grabbed her coat and marched off, taking her sandwich with her. She brushed past a server carrying a tray of food and disappeared around the corner.

"Please forgive me for being rude," Joz said to the man. "It feels so wrong to be nasty to anyone. I hope I'm not like that once my memory returns."

The man's wonderful smile returned. "Young lady, you did me quite the favor. If I had to spend another minute with that pompous woman, I would run back into the fire. Her attitude wore me to a frazzle."

"Me too." Joz giggled. "And I was only around her for a few minutes."

"I enjoy your melodic laugh. Would you mind if this scarred soul sat with you? Perhaps we could split a dessert."

"I would be honored."

Their waitress reappeared then, looking puzzled.

The man beckoned her over and explained that the other woman had gotten called away. He turned to Joz.

"What sweet would you like?" he asked.

"I'm supposed to eat liquid or soft food, and crème brûlée falls into that category," she said hopefully. "Though I can't eat much..."

"My dear woman, you picked my favorite." He turned to the waitress. "One crème brûlée and two spoons, please."

"Certainly. Coffee with that?" she said, addressing both of them.

Oh, you're speaking to me now. "Not for me, thanks."

"Bring a bottle of the finest chardonnay in the house," the man said with a twinkle in his eye and unbridled joy in his voice.

"Yes, sir," the waitress said, starting away. "Right away."

"Young lady—"

Young lady. That sounds familiar too.

"—despite your amnesia, you learned that you're an adventurous woman."

"In what way?" Joz asked.

"You sit with an unkempt stranger, willing to enjoy dessert and wine. That takes strength and no small measure of self-assuredness."

"That's good to know," Joz said, feeling herself blush. "The psychiatrist will probe me this afternoon—I'll bring that up."

The waitress brought the wine first, placing glasses in front of them and pouring. Right behind her was a young man with their dessert. The long-haired man—whose name Joz still didn't know—proposed a toast once they were alone.

"Cheers," he said. "To having been through the wars and surviving."

There's that phrase again. She clinked his glass and drank up.

****

Joz, feeling a warm glow after her second glass of wine, clung tightly to the sense that she had a connection to this man. What it was, she didn't know, but she felt more and more confident it would come to her. Whatever his own memory failings were, he knew a great deal about London and promised, when she mentioned wanting to ride in a double-decker, that he would love nothing more than to ride with her.

"I see you looking at the clock behind me. I don't want to make you late for your appointment," he said.

"I hope we can continue our visit," Joz said hopefully.

"Of course. I absolutely insist." He focused on her walker. "You didn't get from Royal District Hospital all the way here on foot, did you?"

Joz laughed. "Oh, no! I hailed a taxi—his card is in my purse."

"Nonsense," the man said. "I shall drive you. I would never be able to live with myself if something happened to you."

"You've been so kind. There's no need for you to do that."

He pushed on the table and got to his feet. "I insist, young lady. I parked my car at the curb. You can't quite see it from here," he said, looking out the window, "but it's just a few steps away."

"Okay, if you're sure it won't be any trouble…"

Joz managed to stand, but the surroundings seemed to spin.

Then everything went dark.

Chapter Thirty-Three

Joz blinked several times. It took a second to realize she was in the stranger's arms. A uniformed EMT was standing a foot away. Gawkers were being kept at bay by a uniformed police officer.

"You frightened me, Jozelyn." Her new friend paused, eyes widening as if he'd made a breakthrough. "Your name *is* Jozelyn... or is it?"

"Did I faint?" she asked.

"Yes," he said.

She started to ask the man if she knew him, but the EMT stepped forward and wrapped a blood pressure cuff around her upper arm before helping the man get her back into her chair. Joz didn't think much time had passed while she was out, though she couldn't be sure.

"Do you know where you are?" the EMT asked.

"I'm fine—I had lunch here," Joz said, feeling the pinch as the cuff tightened. "Just stood too fast, that's all."

"How much wine did you have," the EMT asked, glancing at the half-full bottle of chardonnay.

"Not even two glasses," the stranger said emphatically.

"Your blood pressure is quite low enough to concern me. Perhaps we should take you in—"

"No, please don't put me in the hospital. Just get me

back on my feet. I have a doctor's appointment to get to."

"You heard her," the stranger said.

"Mrs. Bigelow… oh, my, what happened?"

Recognizing the voice, Joz turned and was surprised to see Tony.

"I came to see what all the commotion was about," he said, "and when I saw your walker—"

"I'm fine, Tony, thank you. I do have a pressing appointment—"

"To which I will drive you," the stranger said. "I insist, Jozelyn."

"Are you sure you don't want to be checked out at the hospital?" the EMT asked.

"No, thank you. But I would like to visit the restroom," Joz said.

The waitress, seating two people at the table offered to lead Joz that way.

"Would you mind holding my coat?" Joz asked the man while reaching for her walker.

"I shall be happy to, my dear."

****

Tony stepped closer. "Sir *Loveland?* What's happened to you?"

"I was in an accident," Frank said to Tony when Joz was out of earshot, motioning for him to sit down. "A fire, if you must know."

"Gracious, Sir Loveland. I will find a product to tone down the scarring if you would like my help."

"That's kind of you, but please refrain from using my name," he said quietly. "I'm incognito—government business."

"Certainly, sir. How do you know Mrs. Bigelow?"

Frank felt a jolt inside him. "Did you say Bigelow?"

"Yes, that's Mrs. Bigelow, recently widowed. She shopped before lunch. I have a sizable delivery to make to her this afternoon."

"A close friend's name is Bigelow," Frank murmured, thinking about Jozelyn's comment that she was from Montana.

"She's a sweet lady," Tony said. "And the poor woman can't remember anything—only knows her name from her passport and credit card." He lowered his voice. "She has amazing credit, I must say."

"Is that so?" Frank began going through the pockets of the coat.

"Uh, should you be doing that, Sir Loveland?"

"I plan to solve this mystery, not steal anything—" Frank's breath caught when he opened Joz's passport. "Mrs. Buck Bigelow," he mouthed, as if trying out the words. "Tony, are you sure she's widowed?"

"She told me so, sir, although she doesn't remember him. According to Mrs. Bigelow, he died in the crash while saving her life. Did you know the man?"

"Indeed! Buck is my trusted and dearest mate, a true brother. I meant to contact him, but memory and health issues plague me."

"Then my sincerest condolences…"

Frank squinted in concentration. *Think!* "Buck was a widower for two years, and not the type of man to meet someone new and then run off. He had no one in his life when we last spoke." He drummed his fingers on the table. "I *must* get to the bottom of this."

"Sir Loveland, didn't you choose this coat?" Tony asked. "I am certain you placed the order from the islands. I found a supplier close to Montana who sent it express. I remember because I have always wanted to meet a Montana cowboy."

Frank ignored the comment. "Find that receipt, Tony. I must have it."

"I will—and this is exciting!" Tony clapped his hands in that irritating way of his. "Two amnesiacs meet at a London restaurant and learn they know each other. How providential—" He covered his mouth. "I am being *so* disrespectful considering your friend's death. I do hope and pray something good comes from it, and I shall contact billing about the receipt and tell them the information is for you."

"No," Frank said firmly. "Do not tell *anyone* it is for me. The facial hair is not the disguise I hoped it would be, and if anyone asks, you have not seen me. It is absolutely imperative, Tony, that you understand this. Do I have your word?"

"Of course, Sir Loveland, I mean Mr. …"

Tony stood abruptly. Frank looked up and saw Joz returning.

"I shall see you in a couple of hours with your purchases, Mrs. Bigelow." Tony held her chair for her. He turned to Frank. "Nice to see you again, sir."

Chapter Thirty-Four

"I never got your name," Joz said once she was buckled inside the long-haired man's Jaguar. As he promised, it was just steps to his car from a side door of the bistro on the east side of Harrod's, and he was a perfect gentleman, opening the door for her before stowing her walker on the back seat.

"My name is Frank," he said, more businesslike than in the restaurant. "And I have made a discovery: your husband is my best friend."

"He is? How is that possible?"

"I am talking about the man listed on your passport—I took the liberty of glancing at it. I shall investigate his death."

She studied the man next to her. The scarring was quite bad above his beard and stunning eyes. "You seem familiar to me, Frank... *so* familiar... I just can't..."

"At the risk of being abrupt, Jozelyn, you could be in danger."

"Danger? From *what?* Whom?"

He drove aggressively and swung onto a side street with no warning. She'd paid little attention to the route her driver took to Harrod's this morning, but it appeared Frank was taking a different way back to her room.

"Danger, Frank?" she asked again.

"Let's get you back to your quarters first. Can you

handle a gun?"

It hit Joz all at once that she'd taken a huge chance by getting into a car with this stranger, not to mention drinking with him. Were they even going to her room?

"Maybe you need to pull over and let me out."

He came to a smooth stop at a traffic light and turned to her. "Communists believe me to be dead, and they know Buck and I were very close associates. They believe in *eliminating* loose ends—and Buck and most likely his wife would be considered loose ends. That would be you."

"Does this have something to do with the accident you suffered?"

Frank moved forward when the light turned green. "I was in a boating accident. That is all I am at liberty to say. But yes, they think I died in the accident." He slowed and made another turn. "We should be right around the corner, Jozelyn, and I insist on not only getting you inside, but confirming the level of safety you have here."

She relaxed a bit as the hospital came into view and was already unbuckling her seatbelt before the car was completely stopped. "There is no need for that. Thank you for a lovely visit—"

He placed a gentle hand on her arm. "Please. I would never, ever hurt you."

Joz looked into his eyes. He struck her as tense, but the same kindness that touched her soul so deeply at the bistro was there.

"Okay, I guess. I would appreciate the help getting inside. I'm tired."

****

She stood near the door, the walker between them,

after he followed her into the room and inspected it. "You scared me when we were in traffic."

"I know I did, Jozelyn—"

"You keep calling me that. Is that my name?"

He looked out the window, then turned to face her. "You cannot stay here. This tiny room with exactly one way in and out, a window that has not been opened in so long it might as well be glued shut."

"Not to be rude, but you don't understand. I have nowhere to go!"

"You shall go undercover with me."

"Good one, Frank. Your wife, the charming *Rose*, would love that."

"I do not live with her, my dear." He stepped over and put his hand on her cheek. "I bumped into her at an art gallery this morning. She saw right through the beard, mustache, and hair in all directions—you have an odd look on your face. What is it? Ask anything you want."

"Would a fire cause amnesia?"

"Clever girl. It was not all from the blaze, though I remained in shock for some time. Look, I suppose you know Buck's former occupation…?"

"I'm sorry. I have no idea."

"Of course," he said, turning red in embarrassment. "In our line of governmental work, wiping memories clean takes place out of necessity. Rose must have been cleared from my mind. Which, is something to be thankful for."

Joz laughed heartily. "I sure wouldn't want to remember her. Though you two must have gotten along at some point…?"

"My employers may have required the marriage. Anyway, please let me move you into my flat for the time being. It is safe, and Jozelyn, I give you my solemn vow I won't hurt you."

She looked into his eyes again and felt she could trust him. "I believe you won't hurt me," she said softly. "And if you truly believe I'm in danger here, I'll go with you. But I must keep that appointment. It's in five minutes."

"How long do you expect it to take?"

"No more than an hour. I'll come straight back and get my things ready. And please take my husband's coat and boots since you're here. It'll be less for me to carry later."

Frank nodded. "I shall be back in an hour."

"Okay. If you're sure all this is a good idea."

"Oh, but it is, my dear." He moved the walker aside and hugged her gently. "Before you object to handling the gun I have for you, I am *certain* Buck taught you how to use a firearm. Something tells me you shall recall what to do if needed."

It feels so good in his arms… and so familiar…

"You truly think that will be necessary? I'm trusting you…"

"Yes, Jozelyn. Better safe than sorry. And I am trusting that it will feel as natural in your hands as you do in my arms."

****

"Good afternoon, Mrs. Bigelow," Dr. Ahmed said. "Please have a seat."

Joz sat on an upholstered couch and sank into it. The office was small and cramped, with reference books in wooden shelving and several framed diplomas affixed to the bland, cinder-block walls. A healthy potted plant sat on the sill of the lone window, which blocked the doctor's view of the brick building several yards away. She remained behind a desk covered in files and reached behind her for a spiral notebook and a small recorder, placed them in front of her, and clicked a button on the recorder. She then opened the notebook to a fresh page.

"So. How are you faring as an outpatient, Mrs. Bigelow?"

"Okay, I guess. I tire easily and must be careful if I stand quickly," she said with a rueful smile. "But I'm glad to be moving around."

Dr Ahmed frowned. "Did you have an outing of some kind today?"

Might as well tell her. "It was the strangest thing. I met a man who knew my husband. He didn't know Mr. Bigelow had died and seemed very distraught."

Dr. Ahmed scribbled in a shorthand only she understood, writing furiously even though the recorder was running. "So the man knew you, too, then."

"That's why this is so weird, Doctor. He *didn't* know me... because he suffers from amnesia, too!"

"Hmm. That is most interesting."

"Yes. See, he had an accident—" *She doesn't need to know it was on a boat.* "—that burned his arms and face. It scarred him horribly, but he has such kind eyes. Those eyes are so familiar. It was like we'd known one another."

"Go on."

She sure doesn't need to know about the wine. "We had a bite to eat at a bistro inside Harrod's—"

Dr. Ahmed's eyes bulged. "You went to Harrod's? Please, Mrs. Bigelow, give yourself some time to regain your strength."

Joz sighed. "That's probably what led me to

fainting. I stood up too fast, and I was in his arms when I came to."

"I must be honest: this concerns me greatly, Mrs. Bigelow. A lot of tricksters, shall we say, are out there. I caution you not to—"

"Doctor, waking up in his arms felt as natural as if I belonged there. And there's more—he called me Jozelyn. My sales attendant at Harrod's knew him, too. They were quite friendly."

Dr. Ahmed stopped writing and looked up. "I am utterly amazed you went clothes shopping let alone …"

"I couldn't come in here looking like something the cat dragged in." Joz smiled sweetly. "And Tony did all the legwork. I tried on several outfits, but I spent the majority of my time in Harrod's sitting in a very comfortable chair sipping coffee."

"Did anything else jog your memory?"

"I haven't had a breakthrough, if that's what you mean, but Frank seems so familiar…"

"The man who claims to know your deceased husband."

"Yes, and I've decided to join him at his apartment instead of staying at the visitor's center. So please give my room to someone else."

Dr. Ahmed sat up straight and leaned toward Joz. Real alarm was in her eyes. "I cannot stop you from doing that. But I strongly urge—"

"I appreciate your concern, Doctor. But I trust this man completely."

"You understand, Mrs. Bigelow, that you are blindly trusting a stranger?"

"My salesperson at Harrod's knows him."

"Fine." Dr. Ahmed was poised to write again.

"Frank… last name?"

"I'm sorry, I didn't get his last name."

Joz could tell Dr. Ahmed didn't believe her, but she didn't push it. "Well, you do seem in much better spirits, I must say. Just be careful, Mrs. Bigelow."

"Of course. And thank you for your concern."

Dr. Ahmed turned off the recorder. "We shall stop here for now. I want to speak with your neurosurgeon before we meet again, which I would like to do next week at this time. Let's agree on six weekly sessions before we turn you completely loose."

"Absolutely. And I'll call right away if the memory bank breaks open."

"Yes, and be on time for your appointment with your neurosurgeon, please."

Joz got carefully to her feet and leaned on her walker. "What appointment are you talking about? Nobody mentioned one to me."

"Well. Then I am glad I did." Dr. Ahmed opened a drawer in the desk and plucked two small cards. She wrote hurriedly on them before handing them to Joz. "Appointment reminders: the neurosurgeon is tomorrow at one o'clock, and next week with me at this time."

"Got it."

"Please rest this evening, Mrs. Bigelow," she added, coming around the desk. "Definitely continue taking your anti-inflammatories and blood thinners. Any questions?"

"One you probably can't answer yet: is my memory loss physical, or an emotional one?"

"That is what we aim to find out." Dr. Ahmed opened the door for Joz. "I hope tomorrow's appointment goes well, and I shall see you in a week."

Chapter Thirty-Five

As Joz reached her room, Tony was hustling up the walk. He held a Harrod's clothing bag in one hand, expertly keeping it off the ground while tugging a plaid gray suitcase with the other.

"Oh, what great timing." Joz leaned on her walker, trying to catch her breath, which fogged in front of her. It was still frigid outside. "May I ask a favor, Tony?"

"Anything, Mrs. Bigelow."

"Would you pack the clothes for me? I'm too exhausted to move."

"Oh? Leaving so soon?"

Joz unlocked the door, stepped into the room, and stood aside to let Tony enter. "Yes. I'll be staying with Frank."

Tony looked at her in surprise. Joz felt herself blush deeply. "Not in that way. He knows my husband."

"Okay, then. Yes, I can certainly help you pack, Mrs. Bigelow." He moved to the bed and set the suitcase down, popping the locks and opening it.

"Those look lovely," Joz said over his shoulder. A leather purse inside matched her coat, boots, and hat. "I love the pocketbook."

"I am certain you shall love all of it, and I am relieved you will not be alone. I memorized Sir Loveland's address and will gladly bring the remainder of your things to his flat—"

"No need for that, Tony."

Joz whirled at Frank's voice, which sounded tense. He'd eased open the door so quietly neither she nor Tony heard him. One of his hands was behind his back.

"Frank," she said carefully, "is something wrong? Tony is here with my clothes—"

Tony turned to Joz. "Not all of them, Mrs. Bigelow. I am terribly sorry, but our seamstress had a death in the family and will be away for a few days."

"I shall pick them up when they are ready." Frank stepped close to Tony. "And I direct you to delete my name from your file."

Joz had no idea what any of this was about and felt a degree of fear. She watched Tony remove a receipt from the interior pocket of his jacket and hand it to Frank. The clothing attendant had a troubled look on his face.

"Here is what you requested, sir, and I must ask if I have done something to offend you…?"

"No, but remember that government secrets *must* be kept confidential. If anyone asks, you heard that I died in a boating accident. This is *extremely* important. And I shall make it worth your while if you notify me of anyone who questions my whereabouts."

"My lips are sealed, sir." Tony turned to Joz. "Thank you for understanding, Mrs. Bigelow. Your purchases will be at the top of the list for our seamstress when she returns. You have my card, and three outfits are in the suitcase—"

"She will be fine, Tony," Frank said. Still keeping his arm from sight, he stepped over to the door and opened it. "Please delete my file right away."

Tony promised he would and walked hurriedly out. Frank shut the door again, only then bringing his hand from behind his back. It was empty.

"Frank, I was hoping to have showered and changed before you picked me up," Joz said. She was still leaning on her walker. "And if I may, what was that all about? You seemed very suspicious of him."

"Tony doesn't need to know the location of my flat, which has been in the family for generations." Frank moved the walker and pulled her to him. "My facilities will be much more to your liking—shower there. Let's get you straight home. Your rest and safety concern me."

"Okay, then. It will only take a minute to pack a toothbrush."

The drive out to the flat took half an hour with Joz relaxing in the plush comfort and smooth ride of the Jaguar. The brick building looked stylish, and she admired the marble walls and gold accents in the lobby before a carpeted elevator took them to the penthouse. Once inside, she gasped at the high ceilings and beautiful view.

"Make yourself at home," Frank said after giving her a quick tour. "The stocked refrigerator and bar are at your disposal. I seldom use the TV, so help yourself. Your room and bath are this way."

"You really expect me to stay in here?" she asked playfully after taking in a spacious bedroom with antique oak furniture and marble countertops. "I'm teasing—it's lovely. It's perfect."

"I am glad you approve. And I am relieved you are here, Jozelyn."

"You keep calling me that—"

"I have no doubt your name is Jozelyn, though I do

not understand *how* I know. If you are uncomfortable with it, my dear, I shall call you Mrs. Bigelow."

She covered her mouth as she yawned. "Jozelyn is a strange name, but it sounds nice—and it's reassuring to have a first name. Maybe we can determine the way you came up with it."

"Maybe we can."

What a wonderful smile he has. "I'll have that shower now."

"I shall prepare tea. See you in a bit."

****

Hurrying to the kitchen, Frank halved his last remaining marinated steak and put it under his broiler, forgetting until the meat was cooking that Joz wasn't supposed to eat solid foods. The more he was around his houseguest, the more attracted he felt toward her, and he had to concentrate on the meal to keep his mind from drifting. He was finishing their salads when it hit him that Joz should have long since finished her shower. He trotted to her bathroom door.

"Jozelyn? Teatime, dear."

He felt a spike of concern roll down his back when she didn't respond. The shower water wasn't running, either. He tried the door, ready to kick it in if she'd locked it for privacy, but it opened right up.

"Dear God," he uttered, discovering her in the tub with water just over her lips. She'd apparently chosen a warm bath and nodded off. "Joz, speak to me!"

Her eyes blinked open. She coughed, trying to sit up. Getting himself soaked, Frank reached into the tub, scooped her out of the water, placed her gently on her feet and wrapped her in a plush towel.

"Frank... I'm so tired."

"You overdid it today. You can eat later. Let's towel off and get you into bed."

****

Frank ate by himself and poured a scotch before settling in a dark gray leather recliner that faced the city lights below. He'd checked on Joz twice, finding her sleeping peacefully both times, and found it increasingly difficult not to climb into bed and take her into his arms.

Why am I thinking such things? I would never cheat with my best friend's wife!

He decided to visit the morgue and ask to view Buck's body—certainly they were waiting for someone to claim it. Then it occurred to him that he could visit the morgue from the comfort of his living room. He reached for his Mac, and a few clicks later he'd easily hacked into the morgue's records. He swiftly confirmed that three were killed in the plane crash, including a man named Buck Bigelow. Frank contained his shock until he read the autopsy results. Then he smiled.

"Buck is no redhead. And that was a short, heavy man who perished, along with two females," he murmured. He got up and poured himself another drink, taking in the majestic nighttime view. "My old friend, you pulled your Casper and ghosted."

Frank was certain that if Buck heard *he* was dead, he'd make certain of it, the way Frank was trying to confirm Buck's supposed death. *What if he looks for me, checking Switzerland's coast to verify my drowning? What if the enemy finds him sniffing around?*

He would need time to think and plan, and that would start with a good night's sleep—he could relax with Joz safe and sound. Before going to bed, he nudged her door open and a jolt shot through him at the sight of her naked atop the sheets. She was holding a pillow in her arms. After studying her and contemplating the undeniable connection between them, Frank covered her with a comforter and pulled the blanket to her chin. She grasped his hand, startling him.

"Frank, come home," she whispered. "Please come home."

He pulled his hand free and staggered across the room, wondering if the scotch had gone to his head. But he'd clearly heard her call his name.

She calls for me, not Buck. Why?

The thought nearly moved him to tears. He crept back to the bed and joined her, fully dressed. He had no intention of undressing and making love to her—not yet—but he felt an urgent need to hold her hand again. He reached gently for her fingers, preparing for a huge letdown if she didn't respond.

She interlocked them with his. And sighed.

He felt a peace inside him he couldn't hope to articulate and closed his eyes.

Chapter Thirty-Six

Briefly disoriented at her surroundings when she awoke the next morning, Joz sat on the edge of the bed trying to collect her thoughts. *What a crazy day yesterday was.* Sandwiched in the middle of the shopping trip to Harrod's and the trip to Frank's flat was the appointment with Dr. Ahmed. The doctor had almost begged Joz not to blindly trust the man who had befriended her at the bistro, and Joz had to admit there were scary moments—such as Frank suddenly looming in the doorway of her visitor's room with an arm behind his back as he stared down Tony, the kind clothing attendant.

Here she was, though, feeling safe and thoroughly cared for by a kind man to whom she felt a deep connection. He felt it, too, she thought, as she found a robe in the closet adjacent to the bathroom. She frowned when she realized how late in the morning it was and hoped Frank hadn't left for work. Grabbing her walker, she opened the bedroom door and went down the hallway. She was relieved to hear sounds coming from the kitchen and smiled when she saw him standing over the stove. His smile nearly melted her.

"Good morning, sunshine. You look lovely," he said. "I was about to check on you—I made soft-boiled eggs and coffee. Cream?"

"Yes, please. I'm starving. I didn't mean to sleep so late."

"Rest and recuperation are exactly what you need." Frank salted and peppered only his eggs. "Remember your doctor's appointment is after lunch?"

"Yes."

"I shall take you. I have errands to run. A bit of this and that."

"Ooh, that sounds mysterious."

"I plan to confirm that Buck, in fact, is alive and well."

About to sip her coffee, Joz paused. "Frank, I understand that Buck was your friend, but he's gone. I have his coat and boots, for heaven's sake."

"I read his autopsy report last night, Jozelyn."

"You did? *How?* I don't even have a copy yet."

"I have my ways. The report indicates that your husband had red hair, was several inches shorter than the Buck I know, and quite rotund."

"You're saying Buck Bigelow isn't all those things?"

He smiled, saying nothing.

"Or are you saying the man in the morgue isn't my husband?"

"I'm saying the mortuary needs a better bookkeeper."

Joz shook her head, confused.

"How about this: when both of us have finished our doctoring, my dear, where in the world would you like to convalesce? Pick a place."

"That's easy... someplace warm. Although dressing in British wool helps, I'd love to feel the sunshine on my face in the morning."

"That sounds enticing. Have you sailed, Joz?"

Turquoise water flashed in her mind. Then it was gone. *Hmm... have I?* "I'm not sure..."

"We shall give it a try in a few weeks when we are both up to standard—a visit to the Canary Islands would be absolutely lovely."

She had a bite of breakfast and a sip of coffee. "There's something familiar about that—I'm wondering if I've been there. You know, it physically hurts my head to try to remember things."

"Give yourself some time. We can work around what you cannot recall."

"Of course, but when I was at Harrod's yesterday I saw several mothers with kids, and it made me wonder about my family. I might have children, Frank—if so, wouldn't they be trying to contact me?"

"Not necessarily. You may be an adventurous type traveling the globe, although your passport shows few entries." Frank tapped his fingers and flashed a smile. "Joz Bigelow, you may not be who you think you are."

"Frank I don't know who I think I am ... that *really* makes my head hurt." She dabbed her mouth with a cloth napkin. "I have a question for you: your real name is Loveland. In your line of work, shouldn't you be a Mr. Smith or Jones?"

"Ah, curious lady, I suggest you research the name. More than one Frank Loveland resides in England—and around the world for that matter. But it was unfortunate running into Tony in Harrod's. I had not lived in England for many years, and it is easy to disappear in a large city if one must. But Tony presents a problem. We had a chat, but I shall fortify it when I pick up your clothes."

This made Joz uneasy. "You won't threaten him or

anything like that, will you? He seems like a very nice person."

"Not at all. It is better to reward than to punish." Frank's phone dinged with a text message. "Speak of the devil…" Frank looked perplexed.

"You're frowning. Something wrong?"

"Tony says your alterations are completed and available for pickup."

"Oh, terrific!"

"The seamstress is away, remember?"

"Yes, but couldn't Tony have sent out the clothes elsewhere?"

"Harrod's does not outsource, period."

Joz shrugged. "Well, since they're ready, can we pick them up on the way to my doctor's appointment?"

"You should wait in the car."

"Frank, I must exercise and breathe fresh air to get well. Besides, I'd love to thank Tony one more time for his kindness yesterday."

Frank opened a drawer. "If you insist, but keep this weapon on you and your eyes sharp. I mean it, Jozelyn. Something about this sounds off."

She thought for a moment. "I can put the gun inside the seat of my walker…"

Frank's eyes twinkled. "What is it, Jozelyn? You have the loveliest smile."

"I think you are right. This gun feels natural in my hand. Maybe Buck did teach me well. I wonder if I've ever shot or killed someone. In self-defense," she added quickly. "What are *you* smiling at?"

"You, Joz. You become more interesting by the minute." He stood and came around the table to her. He bent and kissed her cheek, then helped her to her feet.

"It's good to know I'm interesting. If only I could remember who I was." She looked into his eyes. "I must learn who I am on my own, not by someone pointing it out to me—even if it's you."

"Even if it is me? What does *that* mean?"

"I recognize you intimately, Frank. It's almost like riding a bicycle—you never forget once you learn how, and that's the way I feel about you. You're like a trusted friend, someone I've known forever, although my brain isn't telling me so." She paused, gearing up for what she really wanted to say. "My *body* knows you. When I fainted, you held me in your arms—it felt so natural when I came to. I'm acting like a silly schoolgirl instead of a married woman or widow."

"In what way?"

"Well... I don't like the idea of you leaving on an errand because I'm afraid you won't come home. I *must* be with you today wherever you go. My whole being tells me so."

Frank hugged her so tightly it took her breath away. "You feel as I do. We were deeply involved, Jozelyn."

She nodded into his chest. "I won't know that to be true until my memories return, but I believe it. You represent a connection to my past life, a life preserver that was thrown to me. And I'm not letting go."

Her breath caught as he moved in to kiss her. A shiver went through her body as the familiarity of his taste, scent, and energy washed over her.

"Oh, my," Joz said, feeling dizzy when the kiss ended. He began to open her robe—she was naked underneath—but stopped abruptly. "Frank—what? I was *so* enjoying that..."

"When we make love, my darling, I want my mind

to be totally on you," he said in a raspy voice. "And until we do get those clothes… something worries me about that text from Tony."

She smiled sweetly. "Then we'll wait. When do you want to leave?"

"As soon we can get dressed."

Chapter Thirty-Seven

Frank quieted as they closed in on Harrod's. He had warned Joz they might have to ride around in circles to find a parking place so close to lunch hour, and he finally muttered something she couldn't hear and turned into a parking garage, eventually making his way to the top level. He parked the Jaguar, then took her hand before they got out.

"Let's be careful. I don't know that I suspect Tony, but I'm deeply suspicious for the reason I gave you this morning: Harrod's does not outsource any aspect of their business, ever, for any reason."

"Then do you think—?"

"Let's save our analysis for later. We need to be on our game. That means not just being alert, but keeping your head on a swivel."

Joz swallowed involuntarily. He smiled, maybe reading her mind.

"Again, I am confident you know exactly how to use your weapon, and the hiding place in your walker is perfect. Today we shall take the service elevator to visit Tony. You said you wanted exercise, yes?"

"Yes, I need to move."

Frank hurried to get Joz's walker and help her out of the car. "We want to use those stairs next to the garage elevator—" He pointed behind her. "—as quickly as we can. In this cold, I am gambling that only those who have to be on the stairs will use them, which reduces the number of people who might see us. Just stay as close to me as you can."

They scurried across the garage. Joz had bundled up from head to toe but gloveless so she could grip a weapon effectively. Frank, carrying her walker in one hand as they eased down three flights of dank concrete stairs, gripped her other hand in his. She felt an odd mix of excitement, fear, and love that she looked forward to sharing with him when they were safely back in his flat.

She was breathing hard when they reached the ground floor. Frank pulled her to him as they stood just inside the garage, waiting for her to catch her breath before they proceeded. When she said she was ready, he handed her the walker and led them away from Harrod's front entrance, winding around the block to the building's lower rear entrance.

"This looks like a delivery area," she said.

"That is exactly what it is. Delivery and shipping." Frank stood completely still, craning his head several times to confirm they weren't being watched. Joz felt the frigid cold in her fingers and stuffed them deep in the pockets of her leather coat. She watched several men in matching uniforms unload boxes of product from a panel truck as a woman wearing a pretty scarf and a fur coat gave instructions and marked on a clipboard.

"Let's go," Frank said suddenly.

She followed him, trying to make as little noise with her walker as possible as they hurried past the group—the woman in the fur coat was following the men up into the panel truck to answer a question about the merchandise that was being unloaded, based on a snatch of conversation Joz picked up.

Frank hit a button mounted into a gray concrete wall, opening the service elevator. Once inside, he put his finger to his lips, then hit the button to close the elevator and another for the up arrow. They were alone on the ride, but she knew to be prepared for anything based on Frank's tense body language.

The door opened at the far end of the vast women's apparel section. Joz recognized it and followed Frank past the four dressing rooms. All had doors and, like yesterday, all were closed. An unattended sales counter was a few feet away.

Frank stopped abruptly, hearing something before she did. He tilted his chin back toward the dressing rooms and crept that way, Joz staying close behind.

All hell will break loose if someone sees a man entering one of the—

She froze when she heard a muffled sound behind the second door. Frank, checking over his shoulder, threw it open, his gun drawn. Joz, felt panicked as she tried to stay close. She peered in and saw Tony—he was bound and gagged and taped to a chair. His eyes wide with terror, he shook his head back and forth, almost as if imploring them to run.

"Joz, get inside the elevator," Frank hissed.

He clearly wanted her out of harm's way, but she was using a walker to get around—it wasn't like she was strong enough to sprint out of the twenty feet or so to the service elevator. She also had a purse over her shoulder. Was she supposed to abandon her gun, or open the walker just enough to grab the weapon and carry it in plain sight?

Before she could answer, Frank reacted to a

movement they both heard. He stepped back out of the dressing room and pulled her behind him.

"Throw down gun!" Two menacing Asian men had materialized with guns drawn. As Joz's heart raced, it occurred to her that others might be tied up like Tony. What kind of trap had they walked into?

Frank dropped his revolver to the carpeted floor. Joz knew without him having to say so that she needed to retrieve her weapon—and be prepared to use it at the first opportunity.

"You both come with us," the second man said. His English was as broken as his partner's, but easily understood.

"The lady knows nothing about it, gentlemen."

Joz blinked as an interior lightbulb clicked on. "Oh, dear—" She coughed. "—I'm feeling faint."

"Your inhaler is in your bag, dear."

Frank, she thought, sounded remarkably calm under the circumstances.

"This woman has asthma," he added, addressing the men. "Do you understand me? She will not make it unless she takes her breathing medication."

Joz was hunched down behind Frank's shoulders and couldn't see the faces of their attackers, but this complication may have thrown the men for a loop—a second passed before there was a response.

"Throw bag to me," the first man said. "I take out medicine."

She slipped the purse from her shoulder into her hands as another thought surfaced. "The inhaler is in a green container."

Thrusting the zipped purse up and over Frank, she heard it land in a pair of hands as she flipped open the walker's seat. She removed her gun, flicked off the safety and was about to step around Frank to fire—

"Duck!" A voice behind her shouted.

Frank, whirling, pulled her to him and into a crouch an instant before a shot was fired. The sound was incredibly loud, and Joz saw her purse hit the carpet as the man holding it collapsed, blood leaking from a wound to his chest.

Now!

Ready to blow the second gunman to kingdom come, she sighted him, but Frank shoved her to the floor as he dove for his weapon, which was near her feet. Desperately trying to shield her, he wedged himself in front of her before turning to face the enemy, losing a precious second of time.

BANG!

Though Frank's grunt was barely audible in the immediate aftermath of the shot, Joz felt it physically as if *she'd* taken the bullet. She watched in horror as Frank slid to the carpet, hit in the lower abdomen.

"Now you die," the second communist said, aiming between Joz's eyes. The bastard was *grinning*, and rage ripped through her as she lifted her weapon to kill him.

"I know where the money is," the unidentified shooter said, stepping into view. Something went through Joz—*I know that voice!*—as she watched the man walk calmly, blood streaming from his midsection, hands free and in the air, toward the killer. "Back away from her and—"

Unbelievably, the Asian man turned to look at him while still pointing his gun at Joz. She jerked to the left firing at center mass seeing a red stain bloom on his shirt. In that instant the gunman shot before falling to the

floor—she felt a searing pain on the side of her head—
as she crumpled to the carpet. Then nothing.

"Jozelyn... are you... all right? Buck," he gasped.
"She needs immediate... attention."

An alarm blared, went silent, then repeated.

"I hear sirens, Frank," Buck said. "Hang on—help
is coming."

"I am worried about her," Frank said, gasping. "I
love you, Jozelyn. Don't... leave me."

Chapter Thirty-Eight

Eight Months Later – THE DOUBLE L RANCH

"Senor Bigelow, you catch cold sitting in the evening breeze." Juanita, Julio's wife, placed Buck's coat over his shoulders as he sat on a chair made of rough-hewn timber.

"Juanita, I don't need mothering."

"You do, and Sir Loveland, too. I bring your favorite blanket, Sir Loveland. It keeps you nice and warm."

"Thank you, dear." Frank was next to Buck, his feet propped on an ottoman of sorts made from the same wood. "English wool, you know."

"Critters fed and watered, Senor Bigelow," Julio called out. His face was a mess of dirt and sweat. "I fix the fences today. It was big job."

"I told you to call me Buck."

"Si, Senor. You keep telling me, but I not listen. You build my family a cabin—soon, it is finished. I call you Senor Bigelow forever."

"That is a loyal employee you found," Frank said. "Consider yourself fortunate."

"Maybe, but I'm not used to having this many people under one roof."

"You and me both, my friend, but we need the help."

"Time for medications, gentlemen."

236

Frank looked up as Nurse Jennifer, clad in tight blue jeans with a knit pullover that emphasized her lovely figure, stepped out onto the porch holding a small tray. She took a deep breath of sweet Montana air and beamed at them.

"I shall miss this view and the clean air when I return to London," she said.

"You will not return to England any time soon. We require attention."

"Believe me, Sir Loveland, I do not want to leave, but my visa expires in another month. You have already helped to extend it once."

"Then we shall apply for a green card. What good are connections if Buck and I cannot use them?"

"Sure, Frank," Buck groaned. "Let's build another house while we're at it."

"Don't worry, Mr. Bigelow. I wouldn't be a bother," Nurse Jennifer said, sounding hurt. "I would sleep in the barn if I could stay."

"You shall stay in the house for the duration, and that is final." Frank turned to Buck before looking back at their nurse. "I shall start on the paperwork in the morning. *I will* sleep in the damn barn if that is what it takes to keep you, Jennifer."

"Hold on, now. I wasn't saying you weren't wanted," Buck said emphatically after swallowing a pill. "Forgive me if you took it that way."

"Buck does like you, my dear," Frank said playfully. "But all the trauma changed him. He gets confused easily."

Smiling once again, Jennifer reminded Frank to take his medication and handed him a tiny cup with three pills inside. He waved off the water she offered and swallowed the pills with his whiskey. She said she would check on them later and went back inside the cabin.

"In case I haven't said so lately, Buck, I appreciate you flying me to a London hospital for my burns—private jets cost a fortune," Frank said. "Thing is, I cannot remember anything about that time."

"I'm glad I located you before the commies, partner. Leaving Joz alone to find you in another country wasn't easy for me. Lurking around to find out about your enemies took time, but it saved all of us."

"That it did, Buck."

"As to Jennifer, she proved to be a genuinely caring person when she gave Joz clothes without my instruction and sneaked in that crème brulé like she promised."

Buck sipped his whiskey. "I must say that using an underwater motor and scuba tank wasn't very original—and unlike you. But you managed to get to shore with those injuries. That took fortitude."

"My skin lighting up like a Roman candle after I pushed the ignite button was not a part of my 'unoriginal' plan."

"At least you are officially dead, my friend."

"I was until that Rose woman bumped into me. But I told her she would have to refund the insurance money if she put out word that I was alive."

Buck snorted, sending droplets of whiskey down his chin. "I can't forget that snobby thing. Why did the agency make you two connect?"

"I haven't a clue. But she was essential to me meeting Joz the second time."

"A strange coincidence Dabney would have called providential."

"Ha. I recall Jozelyn using that word."

"I loved having her here, man. She saved me from being a bear's dinner—one gutsy gal—and put a light in my life after Dabney. If she weren't still in love with you, I'd have married her in a heartbeat."

"You are a good fellow, Buck."

Buck clinked Frank's glass with his. "As are you, my friend. We had some good times amid all the craziness, didn't we? And maybe the craziness is in the past. The agency and the newspapers reported you deceased after that last gunfight. The Chinese are no longer chasing you. You ought to change your name."

"I would like to reimburse you for the private jet from Switzerland to London, etc., but I cannot. Let me come clean about something: I signed everything over to Jozelyn in my will." Frank, enjoying the beautiful sunset over the mountains, turned to Buck. "As you say, I am dead and officially broke."

Buck laughed. "I might be able to help, so please forgive an old man whose brain glitched after two operations—and who has a bag hanging on his side—for forgetting a very important item." He pulled off his boot and dug out a key wrapped in paper. "These are the numbers to a Swiss box. I trust you remember Byron, Frank? You sure didn't mention him in your will."

Frank broke into a broad smile, his heart immediately lighter. "Thank God. Your boot seems the safest place for that key. And I shall be glad to split everything with you."

"I know you wouldn't mind donating some acreage. I'd like to start a rescue for the mustangs that the government seems intent on rounding up and slaughtering." Buck returned the key to the boot, and the boot to his foot.

"How American of you," Frank teased.

"Of course—I'd like to update my still and increase production, too. I'm running out of imported whiskey for gifts and bribes."

Frank laughed. "Imported, my big toe. Imported from the Double L Ranch."

"The Montana cowboys believe it, so don't deviate from the story. It's an interesting hobby, my friend, and my product compares to the best. If I keep up production, I don't think they'll question me."

"The phrase 'Montana cowboy' makes me think of Tony. He said he always wanted to meet one."

"That guy in the dressing room who was tied up?" Buck asked. "What became of him?"

"From what I was told, the commies were watching and made their move the morning I got that text from Tony's phone."

"They took it from him, then."

"Yes. Poor boy was questioned but released and, as far as I know, still at Harrod's." Frank pulled the wool blanket tighter around his neck to keep warm.

"One thing I don't get," Buck said. "You haven't explained how you knew Jozelyn after the clearing. That's supposed to be impossible."

"I cannot say I knew her intellectually, but her eyes, her demeanor... something made her seem intensely familiar. Like a dream that sticks to you after you awaken, but you are unable to pinpoint every nuance. She recognized me that way, too, said it was like riding a bike. Our damaged memories failed, but our bodies—our very cells—drew us together instantaneously."

"Strangers enjoying love at first sight, twice, with the same two people—no one claims that distinction. But you must understand by now, brother, that Joz is gone like my Dabney. She's not coming to this time."

Frank felt his good cheer ebb. He stood and stared down at his best friend. "If you insist on being so negative about her health, we shan't discuss it further."

Buck pushed to his feet. "Frank, it's been eight months. Do you really believe Joz wants a feeding tube keeping her alive? Her brain damage is beyond repair, man, irreversible. Let her die in peace and with dignity. Release her."

"My wife breathes on her own. Thank you for relinquishing the master bedroom for her care, but if it is too much of an imposition for you—"

"Now, cut that out," Buck snapped. "Stay until kingdom come, partner, but keep Jozelyn in your heart and get on with your life."

Frank poked him in the chest. "That is what you fail to understand: Jozelyn Hardt Loveland *is* my life, Buck. I shall not release her!"

Both men turned at a sudden commotion coming from the barn. The mules hee-hawed as Diana neighed. James and Bond, snoozing at the edge of the porch, opened their eyes, jumped to their feet, and took off for the open barn door. Buck reached behind him for his rifle.

"It might be a diversion," Frank said. "Stay and protect the women."

Grabbing the gun he kept in his waistband, Frank sprang off the porch and landed stiffly but was able to jog to the barn. He flattened himself against the outside wall and let his eyes adjust to the gathering dusk before peering inside.

Someone—or something—was fussing over Diana.

Or so he thought.

He looked away to regain his bearings, then peered again through the window. A white-haired woman in a nightgown turned toward him, smiling. After a moment he recognized the walker, and finally the catheters that protruded from her neck and arm. He stepped into the barn, praying he wasn't hallucinating.

"Frank," she said, her voice surprisingly strong. "I love the smell and touch of horses. Let's go riding one day."

"Yes, my love," he murmured. "As soon as you feel able."

The doctors reported that the bullet that hit Joz's head jarred her metal plate, causing a stroke that destroyed too many brain functions for her to recover from the coma she lapsed into. But unless his mind was playing an especially cruel trick on him, Frank thought, she was here in the barn and on her feet interacting with horses.

"Jozelyn, I have missed you so." He touched her hair, then her face.

"Don't be silly. You talk to me every night."

Realizing he was still holding his gun, he slipped it back into his waistband when he heard the barn door squeak. "You really heard me, sweetheart?"

"Yes, my wonderful love. Dabney said to rest while my body healed," Joz said. "I returned as soon as I could to care for you and Buck."

"Oh my," Buck said as he and Jennifer walked up. He bent at the waist, beginning to cry.

Jennifer put her arms around him. "The Lord works in mysterious ways, Buck," she said as her eyes watered. "Now, straight away, we must clean and remove those catheters."

"Give me a minute with her, please," Frank said. He moved the walker aside and swept Joz into his arms. "You have returned to me."

"Where else would I be than with you?"

"Indeed, my miraculous love. I have waited for you."

He carried Joz to her room. Jennifer, bringing along the walker, set it next to the bed and washed the straw off Joz's feet after cleaning the insertion sites with antiseptic.

"Must I be in bed, nurse?"

"Only until I dress you in something warmer, Jozelyn. I am not qualified to remove the feeding tube without supervision. We do not want an infection, do we?"

"I called the doc. He's on his way," Buck said hoarsely, walking over to the bed. "He says he has to see this to believe it. Roscoe's driving him—I promised them both whiskey." Wiping his eyes, he took Joz's hand. "Frank never gave up on you, not for a minute. And my New Mexico guests lit candles and are calling a priest to have a special mass of thanks for your miracle tomorrow. I'm so glad those beautiful eyes are open, my friend."

"Anyone who loves touches the creator," Joz said softly. "I learned that while I was away. And I'm so happy to feel all this love."

"People, may I spend some alone time with my Lazarus-love before the doctor arrives?"

"Of course, Frank," Buck said. "I could use another drink."

Frank smiled at his friend, then sat at the edge of

Joz's bed and kissed her tenderly after Buck and Jennifer had left the room. "I must tell you something important," he said, taking her hand. "We enjoyed a rambunctious sex life before, but that is quite impossible for me now with the damage the bullet did when we were ambushed. I will understand if you decide you want someone else, though I fervently hope…"

"I love you far beyond the sex, Frank." Joz squeezed his hand. "I returned to look after you, the way you did for me. Falling asleep in your arms and seeing your face in the morning will still make my world go 'round. We are soulmates."

"You made me a believer in providence. We are pawns in the game of life and love."

"Everything is the way it should be. And will be forever, Frank."

Chapter Thirty-Nine

"Please come home. I love you."

Joz opened her eyes. "Frank... Frank, where are you?"

Erick, holding his mother's hand, sat straight up. "Mom, you came back!" He looked over his shoulder. "Doctor Franks, Mom's awake!"

Joz peered at Erick, recognizing her son but not her surroundings. She was in a hospital room, and a doctor about her age wearing a white lab coat hurried into the room and to her side. Floral displays in varying degrees of health were on counterspace a few feet away, she noticed, along with a TV screen mounted high on the cinder block wall.

"There she is," he said brightly. "Hello, luv."

Joz, looking thoroughly confused and fearful, grabbed the doctor's hand and turned to her son. "Erick, where did you come from?"

"What do you mean, Mom?"

"Frank, we were in Montana. How did I end up in London again?"

"This is a Florida hospital," he said. "Do you remember what happened?"

"You mean the gunman? I saved you and Buck, didn't I?"

The smile he gave her was warm. "I'm Dr. Franks,

your neurosurgeon. Don't worry about your disorientation—you'll make a full recovery. I removed some damaged skull to allow the inflammation to subside. Afterward, I inserted a metal plate in its place. I also fixed a brain bleed and an infection. You had me hopping for a while, but not to worry—you are on the mend."

Perplexed and frightened, Joz let go of the doctor and gripped her son's hand tighter and shook her head no.

"It's okay, Mom. Dr. Franks is the most respected neurosurgeon in the state and promised me he'd heal you. He's saved your life more times than you can imagine."

"What about Buck? He survived the plane crash. Did he live through the gunfire?"

"You were in a car wreck, Mom, not on an airplane. Dad had been drinking and drove straight into the side of a building. A bystander pulled you out after the car caught fire. Thank God he was big enough to yank the door open and lift you out." Erick glanced at the doctor, who nodded for him to continue. "He tried to help Dad and got badly burned. But he assured me that Dad was already dead and didn't suffer. We… we had his funeral and spread his ashes out at sea."

Joz shook her head, unbelieving. "And the man who rescued me?"

"He checked on you after having his burns treated. Buck and I have become friends."

"Buck Bigelow!" Joz opened her eyes wide. "You got to meet Buck?"

"What—no, Buck *Dabson*. I don't think you've met him."

"I don't understand any of this." Joz looked from Erick to the surgeon and back. "Why isn't Frank scarred at all? And why does he pretend to be my doctor?"

"Mrs. Hardt—"

"Please stop calling me that," Joz said sharply. "My name is the same as yours: Loveland."

Erick released his mother's hand and stepped back, a troubled look on his face. The doctor squeezed Erick's shoulder, then sat with Joz and held both her hands in his.

"Sometimes, during unconsciousness, dreams take over," he said gently. "According to scans, you've been experiencing dream after dream for *weeks*. That's why you are confused."

"Oh, God, no," Joz moaned. "It wasn't all a dream. You speak with an English accent!"

"Mom, how can you not remember?" Erick whimpered. "Dad died in the crash—I can't forgive him for almost killing you. You coded *three times* and scared me to death—everyone yelling "clear." If it weren't for Dr. Franks, my anxiety might have killed me. He came into your room during breaks to read Byron to us. I can't say enough good things about him."

Byron. That rings bells.

"Look, Erick… your girlfriend is Alicia. She was here, right?"

His mouth gaped. "How could you know that?"

"I met her at my wedding to Frank. She's a beautiful Chinese girl, isn't she?"

Erick stared and said nothing.

"Why do y'all gawk at me like I'm crazy? Son, you attended my wedding—Peter Maren played at the reception."

"Dr. Franks, my mother has always had movie dreams," Erick said, sounding embarrassed. "Yes, Mom, I'm dating Alicia, and she does have a Chinese heritage—but she comes from Montana."

"Oh, really?"

"Yes, and she's the one. We're dearest friends, soulmates, two pieces of a puzzle. She and I sat at your side for many days. We played your favorite songs in hopes you'd open your eyes."

Dr. Franks turned to the nurse. "Jennifer, sit Jozelyn up for a bit. She'll get a better sense of her surroundings. And make a counseling appointment to help her adjust. That will help your mother tremendously, Erick."

"Nurse Jennifer," Joz said to herself before turning to the woman. "Did you marry Buck?"

"Excuse me?"

Dr. Franks chuckled. "The intensity of your dreams must have come from conversations around you while you were unconscious," he explained. "Our nurse is actually smitten with your rescuer, Buck Dabson—and the attraction goes both ways, I'm happy to say."

Joz felt tears roll down a cheek. "Frank, I don't understand any of this. We're *married*. We're soulmates. How can you act like you've forgotten me?"

Dr. Franks took a second to gather himself, obviously affected by her sincerity. "Jozelyn, I promise that clarity will surface. It will take some time, but you'll get there. Please give it time."

****

Over the next few days, a grim reality began to take hold: everyone insisted that she'd only left Amelia Island in her dreams, and St. Croix was simply a place she once visited on vacation. She deeply grieved as she tried to let go of her unconscious adventures but giving up the life-changing romance with Frank Loveland seemed impossible. The psychiatrist insisted they would never reunite in this reality because he didn't exist in the first place. But Frank lived inside her head and heart.

After she was moved to a regular hospital room, her dearest friends visited and described the night they spent together appealing to God for her recovery.

"We held a vigil for you in Cammy's backyard under a blue moon," Grace said. "It was a beautiful night."

"We burned sage," Jemma said.

"Emma rang bells and copper bowls." Cammy threw back her head and laughed. "My neighbors thought aliens were landing."

"We prayed hard for you," Em said to everyone.

"Each in their own way," Jemma said.

Joz nodded and smiled. "Oh, I remember some of that. You knitted booties for a grandbaby on the way, Emma."

The women looked at each other in stunned silence before staring at Joz with open mouths.

"I only told them a few minutes ago," Emma said in disbelief. "I found out this morning, Joz… and you were in a coma when we had the vigil."

"But I remember! A fire was burning in the pit, Cammy—" Joz turned from her to Jemma. "—and you, Jemma, told me to stay clear of bad boys."

Nobody said anything for a moment.

"We did talk about your tendency to fall for bad boys," Jemma admitted.

"You gals and the doctors call my condition a coma," Joz said. "For me, it was an adventure moving to

St. Croix where I met Frank, a man meant for me and who healed my wounded heart—he taught me to trust. His friend Buck said that love begins with a friendship that's 'solid and true.' "

"Go on, sweetie," Cammy said.

"Being friends with my true love filled the hole in my heart. While you gals were burning sage, I spent over a year somewhere else evolving into a whole human being again, finally moving past the broken heart and ego. So... your vigil must have worked." Joz wiped a tear away. "Thank you, my friends. I love you all."

****

Erick brought a dress, sandals, and makeup on the day Dr. Franks signed her release papers. Climbing unaided into a shower, she smiled as she wondered why men always forgot underwear in these situations. She dressed and arranged a scarf around her head like a turban before covering the circles under her eyes with concealer. She finished applying a hint of color to her lips and cheeks when Dr. Franks stepped into the room.

"Wow!" he said before turning red and offering an apology. "You're recently widowed, Jozelyn, as well as my patient. Please forgive me."

"Nonsense, Dr. Franks. You saved my life. Although I'm sad he died, I don't miss my abusive husband, and I'm flattered by your *wow*."

"In that case, would you consider having dinner with a widower, maybe Saturday night?"

Joz broke into a smile. "I would love to, but don't you think you should tell me your name beforehand? Or should I call you 'Doctor' on our date?"

He laughed, a warm, infectious sound. "Truth is, my parents had an odd sense of humor. It is Francis, but everyone calls me Frank—yes, Frank Franks."

"How interesting! My dream love was Frank, as I told you—here I was calling you Frank when I woke up."

"I'd like to hear more about those dreams over dinner. How about seafood?"

This triggered a memory from a previous conversation. "I prefer seafood."

"Great. I have a special place to take you."

I bet he does. Gosh, what a smile. It could light the planet during a blackout. "Should I meet you there, Frank?"

"I'll pick you up. Erick told me all about your home on the marsh. I'd love to see it."

****

A joyful month of lunch and dinner dates, beach walking, and stargazing followed that first date. The ease of their immediate friendship surprised everyone at the hospital but Erick acted thrilled over the budding romance.

Frank pulled into Joz's winding drive, a lane that took him toward a lush green marsh during high tide. Pink Roseate Spoonbills fed alongside blue herons and wood storks as the sun began to set magnificently on the horizon.

Joz, watching through a gap in the curtains and enjoying Peter Maren's *Dream of Me* on the stereo, smiled as he parked his Jaguar and climbed out. She opened her front door and stepped outside before he rang the bell, and they stood like statues while staring into each other's eyes before she suggested a walk along the marsh before dinner.

The balmy breeze felt wonderful, the familiar earthy scent of the marsh like an old friend. The sunset, she thought, was something out of a Norman Rockwell painting.

"Joz, I would like to discuss something important. I'm not so eloquent with words so please bear with me."

"I'm listening."

"It has been wonderful getting to know you—magical is more the right word. I enjoyed you telling me your dreams about the other Frank. Oddly, I didn't feel jealous of them because I understood that you were truly in love … somewhere else … but your sincerity touched me deeply.

"Now it is my turn, Joz. I need to share an important truth, one I don't understand. But maybe you will."

"Keeping secrets?" she asked playfully while holding onto his arm. "I'm all ears, Frank Franks."

"As you know my wife died over a year ago. We had a good marriage and worked hard to make it work. Really, it was more of a convenience than being a deep love. But friendship does work, and I was at a loss when she died abruptly from a massive stroke that I couldn't fix. That stuck with me for quite a while.

"Strangely, though, at the height of my sorrow, I began to experience recurring dreams that continued for close to a year."

"Oh? What kind of dreams?"

"*You* dreams, Jozelyn."

"What?" She stopped and gazed into his eyes.

"Let me explain. When emergency referred me the night of your accident, the sight of you stunned me. You were the woman in my dreams, but I pushed it from my mind and focused on the surgery." He turned to her. "Jozelyn, you believe that you met me in a dream first somewhere in the Caribbean. The truth is, I envisaged you *before* your coma, before I ever met you. Dream after dream, I saw your face sometimes like it is at this moment... looking up at me, smiling."

"Frank, this is wonderful. Go on. Please," she said as they returned to the deck.

"Other times, we laughed together while walking the beach," he said. "I remembered the turquoise seas, the salt spray, and the moon shining brightly always with you by my side. It is as though someone gave me images to recognize you when you entered my life. And I did.

"As you can imagine, I don't read Byron to all my patients, nor befriend their children. But you were all I could think about; I was consumed, obsessed, smitten. Despite the misgivings of my scientific mind, I believe with all my heart that we did begin a love elsewhere—maybe in another dimension or dimensions where life events intervened and separated us. But somehow, someway, we found each other and our true love—fully awake—in the here and now."

"That's why you believed my coma adventures, then?"

"Yes, but you had to recover slowly. I didn't want to share my truth with you too soon, luv."

She moved close to him and leaned into his shoulder.

"Joz, I am not a superman, nor a secret agent," he began.

"No, but you are more relaxed than the upper-crust Frank in my dreams, and I like it."

"Let me finish, luv. I am no superhero, but I am a successful surgeon of some renown. I don't shoot guns or rifles, but if a fair comes to town, I'll win every stuffed animal for you by throwing darts. I haven't the foggiest idea how to sail, but I own a power boat for fishing. I can't claim any royalty in my bloodline either. Although I'm well off, I'm not super rich, and as far as making love… well, my wife never complained."

She tiptoed and kissed his cheek. "Go on, my Frank."

"We have known each other for a long time if you include other dimensions. I believe we should take our dreams seriously, Jozelyn. Let them take us to the next level—the *forever* level."

Joz nodded with tears in her eyes.

"Will you marry me, Jozelyn, my dream girl?"

She nodded excitedly. "I will marry you in this life and any other."

Frank pulled a small box from his pocket, opening it for her. It was a beautiful yet modest ring of diamond and sapphires. He placed the ring on her finger and kissed her deeply.

Breathless, Joz said, "I've worked up an appetite, Frank. But not for dinner."

"Oh, I agree," he said his body quivering. "I am starving. For my dream girl."

"I'm right here, Frank, falling in love with you for the third time."

"Same goes for me, my luv."

"Maybe we should explore our new reality?" Joz took his hand and opened the front door. Frank closed it behind him while humming their favorite song.

Dream of me. Dream of me.
When you do, I will dream of you.
Every wish you have, I will make true.
When you dream of me.

A word about the author...

Seven Rodgers discovered a passion for writing fiction in 2010. Since then, she has penned five novels and finds writing a natural extension to her eighteen-year career as an entertainer, writing award-winning music and lyrics.

Rodgers attended the University of North Florida, Jacksonville.

She moved from Amelia Island, FL to St. Croix, USVI where she snorkeled, wrestled a fixer upper into submission, and wrote Dream of Me.

Seven has one grown son, Luke, and three stray dogs that adopted her.